This book is lovingly dedicated to my own "brunch club"

I can't name all the women in my life who have loved me, laughed with me, prayed for me, and shared life's challenges along the way.

*You know who you are,
and I am blessed to call each of you "friend."*

THE HARBOR COVE BRUNCH CLUB

Book 1 of the Harbor Cove Series

LAUREL WENSON

Welcome to Gloucester, MA! While this is a work of fiction, the story takes place in a real setting.

Gloucester has been special to me all my life. As a child, our extended family would picnic at Stage Fort Park, and my cousins and I would climb the rocks on Half Moon Beach and Tablet Rock. I toured Hammond Castle, fascinated by the Great Room, the courtyard, and the gorgeous gothic arches overlooking the harbor. My dad's love of boats prompted many visits to the harbor along Stacy Boulevard and Rodgers Street, and I have vivid memories of walking along Pavilion Beach and wondering what the Greasy Pole platform out in the harbor was all about. We walked along the State Pier and around Harbor Cove to admire countless fishing boats, and enjoyed fresh seafood at Woodman's in nearby Essex.

As a young adult, I'd join friends for beach trips to Good Harbor or Wingaersheek, and on my own, I spent countless hours perched out on the breakwater at Eastern Point, or staying overnight at the Cape Ann Motor Inn on Long Beach. Although I haven't been back in many years, I will always love this small fishing community, and it was an easy choice as my series location.

You will find real places and events mentioned in the series − there really is a wonderful fiesta in honor of St. Peter each year, and the Greasy Pole contest is a highlight of the weekend. There is an actual neighborhood known as the "Fort" between Pavilion Beach and Harbor Cove, and documentaries exist to give the history of how it came to be one big "family". Across the harbor, Hammond Castle is still open to the public for tours of magnificent medieval architecture. Along the way, the Fishermen's Monument stands proudly facing the harbor in memory of those who have been lost at sea.

While several locations in the story are real, this is a work of fiction. Please know that some places may not be described exactly as they are in real life. None of the characters are real people, and the story ideas all come from my imagination. For your benefit, I've included a "family" directory at the back of the book; it will make it easy to keep track of each of the brunch club ladies and their children. I hope you enjoy the melding of "real" places with "make believe" characters -- Viva!

For more information about Gloucester, MA, be sure to visit their website at discovergloucester.com

CHAPTER ONE

"There must be a good eight inches of goop on that pole," Sharon surmised as she squinted in the afternoon sun. The local ladies laughed. The beach was packed, all eyes on a wooden platform about two hundred yards out into the harbor. About fifty rowdy men, some dressed in odd costumes, cheered from the top of the platform about twenty feet above the water. A greasy telephone pole protruded horizontally from one side, with a flag mounted at the far end. "It looks like shaving cream."

"Trust me, it's grease," Terri Rossi said, licking her oily fingers as she ripped a piece of fried dough off of the plate beside her. "They throw on every kind they can find – bacon fat, Crisco, fish guts, and God knows what else. Of course, a lot of it comes off during the courtesy round." Holding her plate out, she grinned. "Speaking of grease, want some of this?"

"It smells heavenly," Sharon replied, "but my stomach would hate me later." She watched as another contestant, with flailing arms, plunged into the harbor with a huge splash. "So, all those guys on the platform are gonna try to reach the other end to grab the flag before falling into the harbor?"

Jean McBride's laugh was deep and hearty. "You've summed it up well for a first timer." She reached over to grab some of Terri's offering. "What the hell? It's not fiesta without some greasy food – we'll all gain five pounds this week."

"And spend five months taking it back off," Kelly teased.

Sharon remained fixated on the harbor. "So, what does the winner get?"

Their laughter was louder now.

Betty Sue Marino, who had invited Sharon to tag along to meet the brunch club, reached over to pat her hand. "Don't you worry your pretty little head about them," Betty drawled, "They like to tease sometimes, but they're all as friendly as can be."

Sharon found a little solace in Betty's words. "But seriously, what do they win?"

Kelly Fitzgerald-Doyle, the youngest of the group, replied. "Bragging rights – and plenty of free drinks later on. And after leading the rowdy chant to St. Peter, the losers carry the winner around the neighborhood on their shoulders." She raised her glass for a toast. "Viva!"

The ladies all joined with an echo. "Viva!"

Sharon shook her head as distant strains of carnival tunes ebbed and flowed over the din of the crowd. "I'm not sure I understand any of it, but I bet it's gonna be entertaining." She chuckled as another couple of contestants slid out and fell off the pole as the crowd cheered and boat horns blared. One was dressed like a mermaid, and the other a superhero. "Do they at least have a prize for best costume?"

"A small cash prize," replied Arlene Winston, the quietest of the group. "Almost all of them are part of the fishing community here, and this whole Fiesta is in honor of St. Peter, the patron saint of fishermen. The only thing more important than family and fishing to them is their faith. They bless the fleet this weekend and everyone prays for the safety of each crew. Goes back to 1927."

The crowd cheered louder as one contestant made it out three quarters of the distance to the flag. Sharon winced as someone nearby blasted an air horn and yelled "Viva!" along with his friends.

"Terry, you said Bill was competing this year?"

The oldest of the group nodded. "He's wearing bright yellow shorts and a navy-blue tee shirt. I hope he wins."

Betty Sue agreed as she filled Sharon's glass with more wine. "Bill fishes with Terry's husband Nate. Terri's son Anthony won the Greasy Pole contest six years ago."

Sharon turned toward the older woman, who was watching for Bill to emerge on the pole out in the harbor. "So, Terry, is your son out there?"

All conversation stopped as all eyes veered toward Sharon. Terri said nothing, her stoic gaze staring far beyond the Greasy Pole platform. Her voice croaked a bit when she replied. "Yeah… he's out there." An awkward silence permeated the group as Terri stood up with a pained sigh and brushed the sand off of her shorts. "Gotta check on Nate − he's working the Elks tent at the end of the beach. You guys can finish the funnel cake."

"I'll go with you," Arlene said jumping up. "James will be looking for me shortly and I told him I wouldn't keep him waiting."

As they trudged off, Sharon shook her head. "Can someone please tell me what the hell I said to offend her?"

Betty Sue patted her hand again. "Aw, sweetie, it's okay. You didn't know."

"I didn't know what?"

Jean finished her drink. "Terri's son was lost at sea three years ago. This is always a tough weekend for her. For all of us, really. Anthony was a great guy."

"That's right," Kelly continued. "And Anthony was all set to marry Jean's daughter Kim before he died." She turned to Jean. "How's Kim doing these days?"

"Some days are good, and others are tough. She still refuses to show up for the Fiesta. Too many memories."

"That's understandable. There's a lifetime of memories on this beach."

"I'm sorry about Kim's loss as well. You guys are so close; did you all grow up here in Gloucester?" Sharon asked.

Jean nodded. "Most of us grew up right behind us, in the Fort."

"The...fort?" Sharon scanned the horizon beyond, seeing nothing but a large hotel, fiesta rides, and assorted rooftops.

"The real fort is long gone," Betty Sue drawled, "But the Fort is the neighborhood between the beach and Harbor Cove on the other side —mostly Italian fishing families. Jean, Terri, and I grew up there."

Kelly continued. "Terri moved out when she got married, but Jean and Betty's mom are still in the same houses their grandparents lived in."

"What about you and Arlene?" Sharon asked.

Kelly chuckled. "I lived up off of Main Street, where some looked down on the Fort kids. When I became friends with Betty Sue and started visiting down here, I was envious of what they had – like one big family."

"Yeah, she was adopted by us," Jean said. "And later on, Peg and Arlene joined us, and at some point, we dubbed ourselves the Harbor Cove Brunch Club. We used to lug everything we needed for proper brunch celebrations all the way over here – people said we were nuts."

"We stopped the fancy table set up years ago," Kelly pointed out. "I think it would kill us now."

They were interrupted by Betty Sue. "Hey, I think the competition round is starting!"

A cheer rose from the crowd as the first contestant awkwardly slid a few yards out onto the pole, waving his arms wildly as he splashed into the harbor below. Sharon noted almost as many spectators out in boats as on the shore, and the cacophony of horns grew louder as contestants got closer to the flag, followed by the moan of the crowds as they hit the water below.

Betty's phone rang. "Oh, Lord, what does she want now?" She spoke loudly over the noise of the crowd. "Hello, mother...what's the matter?" She rolled her eyes as she listened. "There's nothing wrong – she'll be home later. I told you this morning Carla's working late and won't be home for dinner."

Kelly leaned in toward Sharon as the call continued. "Her mom has dementia, so she forgets a lot these days."

Sharon nodded with understanding. "I imagine that's hard. But does she live with her at the townhouse? I don't remember ever seeing her."

Jean shook her head. "She lives right across the street from me. Betty's daughter Carla lives with her and keeps an eye on her at night, and my daughter Hannah watches her during the day."

Betty ended her call and finished the last of her drink, grabbing the plate of funnel cake and stuffing a large piece into her mouth. "I swear she's driving me crazy," she mumbled. "I think she's called ten times today wondering where Carla was. Sounds like they filled you in."

"They did – and I'm sorry for what you'll deal with down the road. Alzheimer's is a nasty disease."

"You're not kidding. And today she's in rare form since she's home alone. I may have to stop by on my way to dinner." Noting the powdered sugar on her fingers, she dropped the plate. "Oh, shit, and now she has me stuffing my face. I'll gain five pounds from this alone."

Kelly grinned. "You seeing your new beau again? You'll exercise it off later tonight. I thought you were gonna drag him along with you today."

Betty blushed. "Aw, don't you worry your pretty little head about that – I've decided to throw a little brunch in a couple of weeks so all of you can finally meet him. Sharon, you'll have to drive back up that weekend – I hope you can come."

"We can chat before I head home later—"

"Oh, there's Bill!" Jean interrupted. They watched as the next fisherman almost danced across the pole. He lost his balance as he neared the far end, but extended his arm frantically and managed to snag the flag as he fell to the water below. Applause and cheers broke out throughout the crowd along with a chorus of boat horns.

"Viva!" Kelly yelled out along with those around her. "Good for him! Terri and Nate will be so happy."

Sharon watched as all the remaining men on the platform joined the others who had fallen before, and the entire group swam to the shore as Bill awkwardly dog paddled in with one hand as he held the flag above the water. "Well, that was definitely not something you see every day. But now I can go home and tell Dad all about it. He noticed the platform his first visit up here and wondered what the heck it was for."

"How far away are you?" Jean asked.

"About an hour. We're from Caldwell – about twenty minutes west of Boston."

"And she's coming back again in two weeks," Betty insisted. "I tell you, Sharon, you simply have to be here so you can all finally meet my new sweetie. I swear to you ladies, he is the *perfect* man!"

Sharon pasted a smile on her face rather than reply. *There ain't no such thing, lady. But maybe I'll come back up to be entertained. Besides, I like these women.*

CHAPTER TWO

The following morning Jean McBride was in her studio early. The fiesta energized her each year to paint harbor scenes – some of the fiesta and others of various spots she knew in her head. Something about being on the beach all day with friends and listening to the "Viva!" chants throughout the crowd. She had lightly sketched the Greasy Pole platform before grabbing her paintbrush, and tried to capture Bill as he grabbed the pole in the air.

By the time Hannah popped in she had the basic form done and was working on the harbor and boats before tackling the platform itself. "Morning, mom. Brought you another mug of coffee." Hannah was a natural beauty with long blonde hair and blue eyes peeking out from under a Patriots baseball cap. She had on shorts and a "Viva!" tee shirt as she placed the mug on her mom's "coffee" stool.

Jean reached for it as Hannah picked up the empty mug. "Thanks, honey. Got out here early this morning. Did you sleep in that?"

"No – yesterday was a white shirt. Today's is yellow in honor of Bill's fluorescent shorts. I thought the folks at adult daycare would enjoy it. We'll do lots of reminiscing today, I'm sure." She looked over her mom's shoulder. "You need a show someday with all your Fiesta paintings – could probably make a fortune."

Jean leaned back as she studied her work. "Not a bad idea – I could rent space at the communal gallery out on Rocky Neck next year. You heading over to pick up Elena?"

Hannah looked at the clock on the wall. "In about ten minutes. Thought I'd check in since I was out later than normal. Your light was already off when I got home so I didn't say good night."

"I think the fresh air and excitement did me in – and the wine. Was a gorgeous day. Did you go out with Carla last night?"

"Hell, no – I hung out with her and some of the others on the beach, but they were going bar hopping with the guys afterwards. Definitely not my thing. I actually hung out with Vinny all evening – he was taking tons of photos for Peg to use in her column today."

"Did he talk to his folks at all? I know Nate was working the Elks tent, and Terri joined him later. I wish they could reconcile."

"He spotted his dad, but they didn't talk at all. Terri might have spoken to him if they'd run into each other." Hannah leaned forward and rested her elbows on the end of Jean's work table. "I don't understand how his folks can love others so much and yet turn their back on their only remaining son – just because he's gay. It's so wrong."

"I suspect his sexuality is only a part of the problem. He made it clear long before he came out that he had no desire to join Anthony and his dad on the boat. I don't think Nate's forgiven him yet."

"Well, he's sure rubbed it in Vinny's face over the years. Bill is more of a son than he is – especially since they lost Anthony." Hannah was quiet for a moment. "How was Kim last night?"

"The usual. She spent the day over at Hammond Castle getting ready for a few tours this week, and came home trying to pretend it wasn't Fiesta weekend. She cried when I told her Bill won."

"Jeez, I wish she'd open up and let him in. Bill's been head over heels in love with her forever, and she's got walls up as thick as the castle she spends her summer in. Is she ever gonna be herself again?"

Jean sighed. "Everyone grieves at their own pace, honey. And even when she heals from losing Anthony, there's still the fear of being with another fisherman. I hope Bill keeps trying to chip away at that wall. He'd be perfect for her."

"I'll offer her a Tarot reading tonight if she's up for it. In the meantime, I gotta pick up Elena and head to work. I'll be home for dinner, and can tell you all about Vinny's place – did you know he's living with Peg now, along with two other boarders? Such a peaceful vibe."

"Sure it's not all the cats?"

Hannah laughed. "She really *is* a crazy cat lady – just adopted another black cat named Mitzi. That makes nine ."

"Oh, my Lord. Don't get any ideas. Java and Grandma Moses are quite enough for this household."

"Don't worry, mom. I can head over there anytime I need a real cat fix. Get back to work on your latest masterpiece and you can show me tonight!"

Hannah crossed the street, picking up a few pieces of trash along the sidewalk left behind by Fiesta revelers and walked around the aging Cape Cod to the back door. She knocked three times and opened it with the key Elena had given her. "Elena! It's Hannah!" She introduced herself the same way every morning, as routine was important to Elena's care, and Hannah didn't want to scare her by wandering in unannounced.

The older woman was wiping down the kitchen table with a ratty old dishtowel. Hannah winced and wondered where Elena had found it; she had stayed late on Friday to finish up a load of laundry after daycare and hung a clean one on the hook.

"Morning, Elena. Are you all ready to visit your friends?"

Elena smiled from across the table, her face lighting up when she spotted Hannah's tee shirt. "Viva San Pietro!" she cheered, waving her rag in the air. "Is it fiesta time? I need to find my fiesta hat..."

Before she could head into the living room, Hannah stepped in to give her a hug and redirect her. "No, the fiesta's all over, Elena. But we're gonna talk about it all day. You can tell me about your favorite Greasy Pole contest on the way." *Works like a charm.*

They walked the two blocks to the local Methodist church where the adult day program met, and Elena chatted the entire trip about Greasy Pole winners from the 60s and 70s, happy to greet her friends when they arrived. Other staff had worn various Fiesta clothing as well, and before long the entire room was full of laughter and anecdotes.

Hannah loved working with the elderly locals. Almost all of them had spent their lives in Gloucester, and most had worked either on a fishing boat, on the wharf, or in the fish factory. She suspected someday Elena would forget who she was, but still know every other old timer in the place. As she wandered over to prepare a morning snack for everyone, she opened a cabinet door, only to have the bottom hinge let go; the cabinet door slid and banged into the wall. "Damn it!" she muttered, remembering a moment too late about Friday's exact incident.

"Looks like I'm a few seconds too late," a voice said behind her.

She spun around to an attractive guy a little older than she was wearing earbuds. His tattoos announced his arrival to most people, and Hannah noticed a few judgmental expressions from her clients, but she loved the tousled hair, the bristly beard, and the peace sign adorning his neck just above his tee shirt. Both arms had extensive detailed tats on them, and she forced herself to look at his face even though she'd rather study them instead.

"I'm here to fix--well, I'll be damned. Hannah McBride, how are ya?"

"JJ? Oh my God, it's been forever. When did you get back in town?" She knew JJ had dropped out of school at the end of their sophomore year, left town, and experimented with drugs. "And why are you here to fix the cabinet right when I need it?"

She enjoyed hearing JJ's laugh again. He waved to the larger group of ladies now pausing to watch him and held up a screwdriver. "How 'bout I take care of it so you can feed all of them, and then I can fill you in a bit?"

She smiled. "Deal. Let me grab the peanut butter and I'll use the other end of the counter so you can work." She turned to the now silent group. "This is my friend JJ. He stopped by to fix a broken cabinet door. Your snacks will be ready in a jif, okay?" Her reassurance was all they needed, and soon the chatter resumed.

JJ chuckled. "Ready in a jif? Some kind of subliminal advertising?"

He gestured toward the peanut butter and Hannah cracked up when she read the label.

"That was totally unintentional, I swear."

"So, you're still in town, huh? I kinda figured you might have traveled the world or joined the peace corps or something. But I guess you're making the world a better place right here at home." He glanced over as he worked and grinned.

God, she remembered his grin from earlier years. All the girls wanted him – especially Carla. She loved the rebellious type and had a major crush on JJ. Hannah doubted she knew about his return yet, or she would have heard all about it.

"You always so pensive when you're spreading peanut butter on crackers?" JJ was leaning against the counter studying her, and she felt herself blush a bit.

"Only when guys stare at me with a screwdriver in their hand," she teased. "Let me bring these over to the table and I'll be right back."

"I've got a better idea. How 'bout we grab a cup of coffee later on instead? You still living with your mom?"

"I am – and she'd love to see you. She finally retired a couple of years back, but you were always one of her favorites. You could stop by any time after 4:00."

"I work when I leave here, but I finish up at 6:00. Is that too late? I don't wanna wreck any dinner plans."

"There's no set dinner schedule at our house, so come whenever."

JJ tucked the screwdriver into his tool belt. "It'll be nice to say hi to your mom. She was one of the best teachers Gloucester High ever had. I guess I better let you get back to work." As he reached the door he turned back and smiled. "And you might wanna put on pants and long sleeves tonight. It's gonna be cooler than normal, and I've got my bike back."

As she served peanut butter crackers to her clients, her mind was already picturing him arriving on his bike. *Damn. If Carla doesn't know you're back yet, your bike will be a dead giveaway in no time.*

CHAPTER THREE

Hannah dropped Elena back off at home, and after setting her up with coffee and a slice of banana bread to tide her over until Betty Sue stopped by with dinner, she scooted across the street. Kim's car was in the driveway, and she was glad to find her in good spirits in the kitchen.

Kim was several years older and shared the long blonde hair, but she wore dark eyeglasses and didn't smile as easily as Hannah did. "Hey, you're home. Come chop veggies with me – mom suggested kabobs on the grill for dinner."

Hannah planted her bag on the counter and pulled her hair back into a pony tail. "She still painting?"

"Almost done. She started two different scenes today. Says she'll be out within the hour. How was work?"

Hannah grabbed a paring knife and a small zucchini from the pile in front of her. "Interesting."

"Are you gonna elaborate?"

"JJ Winston showed up to fix a broken cabinet; haven't seen him in forever."

Kim put her knife down and grinned. "Do tell. Does he still have that attractive 'bad boy' look?"

"Oh, yeah – kicked up a notch or two."

"And can he still make my little sis blush?"

Hannah grinned. "You can assess that yourself later on. He's picking me up to go grab coffee somewhere and catch up."

"No way!"

"On his bike."

"Oh my God – is Carla home? She'll be beelining it over here as soon as she hears him coming."

"Not sure; and I doubt she knows he's back yet or she would have said something yesterday or texted me last night." Hannah sighed. "I wonder if it will start all over again."

Kim held up the vegetable peeler she was using on a carrot and shook it at her. "Don't you dare let her manipulate you this time around. Just because she wanted him back in high school doesn't mean you have to step aside and let her go after him again."

Hannah remembered numerous spats with her best friend before JJ left town. Any time JJ gave her attention Carla spouted off about the girlfriend code of crush boundaries. "I have dibs on JJ," she'd insist. "Besides, he's not your type; I'm the one who likes the bad boys."

"She still prefers the rebel types, doesn't she?"

Kim shook her head. "I think they prefer her – she's way too easy when she's drunk. And that one night she had with JJ doesn't mean shit today."

"Jeez, lay off! We're only having coffee, for God's sake."

Kim opened a package of wooden skewers. "I still say he's always been interested in you. Don't let the past limit the possibilities, that's all."

Hannah leaned forward. "Well, *you're* one to talk! Isn't it about time you took your own advice?"

Kim glared at her as she stabbed a piece of zucchini. "It's not the same."

"The hell it isn't! We both know that Bill's been in love with you forever. He would have told you if Anthony hadn't won the Greasy Pole contest that day."

"Will you please shut up?"

Hannah was too fired up. "Anthony got drunk enough to make his move that night and you were hanging all over him. So best friend Bill stepped back and watched the two of you fall in love and get engaged."

"I said shut up!" Kim slammed her skewer down on the counter as bits of crumbled mushrooms flew across toward Hannah.

"Whoa – what the hell's going on?" Jean McBride came in from the back hallway wiping her hands on a towel. "I could hear you from the studio."

"Ask her. I lost my appetite!" Kim stormed by and stomped down the hall, slamming her door in the distance.

Jean leaned against the counter and crossed her arms in front of her. "Care to explain?"

Hannah kept her eyes down as she wiped up the mushroom pieces. "I pushed too hard. Should have known better." She gave her mom a quick recap of the conversation.

"Ouch. More like a shove than a push. What were you thinking?"

"I wasn't, okay?" Hannah's tone softened as she met her mom's gaze. "But I hate seeing her so depressed, when Bill could make her happy if she gave him a chance."

"She'll be okay, but the grief process can't be rushed." Jean came over and put her arm around Hannah's shoulder. "I'll go in and talk to her after you leave. But in the meantime, why don't you tell me about JJ? Arlene hasn't said anything about him being back."

Hannah chuckled. "Maybe she needs permission from her master to talk about it."

Jean's laugh lightened the mood once again. "Don't you start, little Miss Sassy Pants. Not all my friends share your feminist views on marriage. Even if I agree with you on this one."

They worked together in silence getting the kabobs finished up, and Hannah offered to grill them and make a salad while Jean changed out of her paint speckled clothes. By the time dinner was ready, the rumble of a motorcycle reached them through the open window.

Hannah yanked the pony tail out of her hair. "Dang! I still need to change."

Jean scooted her down the hall. "I'll get the door; JJ and I can catch up."

By the time she got back to the kitchen Jean was adding another plate to the pile. "I invited him to eat with us before you two head off – there's plenty of kabobs to go around."

JJ grinned as he picked up the tray laden with vibrant colored veggies. "Hope you don't mind. How could I pass up these beauties? Thanks for the invite, Mrs. McBride."

"Please, call me Jean from now on. Why don't you two start and I'll find out if Kim's gonna join us."

Hannah gestured for JJ to sit and handed him the tongs. "These are for the salad. You can grab the kabobs by the skewers. The ones on your end have shrimp, while this end are all veggies."

JJ loaded his plate with salad first and then reached for two skewers closer to Hannah. "Are these okay to take? I'm a vegan now, but I could pick the shrimp off the others."

Hannah grinned as she reached for her own. "A fellow vegan? I remember you as being a burger guy way back when."

"Yeah, a lot's changed over the years. But you – I think you were lecturing your classmates in middle school about saving the animals."

"Guilty as charged. I've been vegan since I was about eight years old and saw the movie *Babe* for the first time. That whole conversation with the cat about pigs and their 'purpose' for life opened my eyes and made me a convert. But what about you?"

"I'm a newbie – only a couple of months now, but man, I feel better." He bit into a grilled piece of zucchini and met Hannah's gaze. "I guess being clean helps a lot, too. I suspect you heard about me being arrested?"

Hannah nodded. "Your mom told my mom awhile back. There was a small bit in the paper when it happened, but then it kinda disappeared."

"Yeah, my dad pulled some strings and tried to keep it quiet – more for his image than mine, I'm sure."

Jean returned alone to hear JJ's comment. "Sounds like you've been doing well in recovery." She glanced at Hannah as she sat down. "Kim's got a headache, so she'll grab a plate later. So, I guess you're back home at this point?"

JJ sighed. "Sometimes it feels like house arrest, not gonna lie. I finally got my bike back on the road, so hopefully I'll be able to escape from time to time – like tonight, for instance." He gazed at the kabobs remaining on the tray. "Think I could snag one more? They're awesome."

Hannah slid the tray closer to him. "Take two. Mom and Kim both eat shrimp."

They chatted until their plates were empty, and JJ leaned back in his seat. "This was the best meal I've had all week. Thanks again, Mrs. Mc—Jean—for having me."

"Stop by any time," Jean replied. "Now why don't you two take off and I'll clean up?"

"Thanks, mom. We won't be too late."

"Damn right," JJ said with a grin. "And who would have thought that I'd be the one with a curfew?"

CHAPTER FOUR

The phone rang as Arlene Winston finished vacuuming the living room. She stepped over the cord and dashed to the kitchen, answering before the third ring. "Winston residence."

"Hey beautiful, what are your plans for later today? I had a client postpone a house viewing and I thought we might hang out." Kelly's voice was always upbeat and to the point.

"I'm not sure. James said he might be working late, but if he doesn't then I'd need to be here to make dinner."

Kelly's disapproval came through loud and clear. "The man can't make a sandwich or grab some leftovers?"

Here she goes, again, telling me why my marriage is horrible. Arlene's thumb fiddled with the wedding ring on her left hand as she spoke. "James doesn't eat leftovers; he prefers a hot meal when he gets home from the office."

"I need to buy you a crockpot, woman — then he can have a hot meal every damn day and you can put a little spontaneity back in your life. When will he enlighten you about his plans?"

You'll never understand my James. You don't even try. "He's in court this morning, so not until lunch. For now, I'm catching up on the house after being at Fiesta this weekend."

"Let me know when you hear from him. I'm in the office for another hour and then have a closing. If I don't pick up, leave a message and I'll call back as soon as I'm done."

"I can't promise anything." *Please don't be mad at me. I really do wanna go.*

"Believe me, I'm well aware of your constraints. But it might entice you a bit to hear the yarn shop is having a sale on those soft skeins you were admiring last time. Might be time to stock up for a new project."

Arlene's voice brightened. "The blue and orange ones? On sale?"

"Not only on sale, but fifty percent off. I gotta run – call me later!"

Oh, that yarn! It's ultra-soft, and would keep me warm while James watches his boring history documentaries. Arlene hung up the phone, praying silently for his meeting to take place. JJ could fend on his own. She grabbed the vacuum and headed for the den, determined to finish cleaning the house – just in case. *Another day out would be a real treat!*

Hours later she was checking her pantry and planning meals for the rest of the week when the phone rang again. "Winston residence."

The curt, gruff voice on the other end increased her anticipation. "I'll be dining with Bruce at the Elks tonight. It's a big case, so I may be late getting home. Be sure to remind JJ of his curfew if he goes out."

"I will, James. I hope you had a productive morning. I got a call from Kelly—"

"Like every other day, it was busy. I need to run."

"Alright, dear. Have a nice afternoon—"

The click cut her off. Never a question about her day, or what her plans might be. *I do love him, Lord, but if only he could...never mind. He's a good provider, and a faithful man – and for that I'm grateful.* A moment later, she realized her afternoon was now free, and she quickly dialed Kelly's number and left a message, as promises of soft yarns and dinner laughter replaced the empty loneliness her husband evoked.

She wrote a note for JJ, reminding him of his curfew and the leftover meatloaf. He loved her meatloaf – always had – even more so the next day in sandwiches. She signed her name and drew a little heart with a cross in it like she always did. *I love you, and so does God.* She'd murmured the same phrase for years – tucking him in at night, handing him his lunch as he headed out the door, leaving notes on the fridge when he stayed out late at night, and later praying for him after he quit school and left home.

As she drove to Kelly's office, she gave thanks he was at least home again and free from drugs. *He could have overdosed or gotten killed in a drug deal. Now he's safe, and starting over. And hopefully James will forgive him someday for all the trouble he caused.*

She parked her car in the last spot away from the road at Kelly's office. While she was happy that Kelly offered to drive, she was always nervous that James would discover her car out and about without his prior knowledge. Her concerns faded as Kelly exited the building with a warm smile on her face.

"Saw you pull in, and I'm more than ready to get out of here. All set?"

Her step quickened and she reached the passenger side of Kelly's car, waiting for the unlocked door click, feeling like a giddy school girl playing hooky for the afternoon. "For another afternoon out? And yarn on *sale?* What do *you* think?"

Kelly grinned as she pulled out of the lot. "I think you need a life, girlfriend. Maybe a job where you can leave the house every day. Imagine that!"

Arlene closed her eyes, content to breathe in the salt air as her friend whisked her away to the outskirts of town. "I *have* a job. And I love taking care of my home."

"I'm well aware; I'm the one who found it for you, remember? And while I'm glad you still love it all these years later, I wish it was a little less of a prison for you sometimes."

Arlene winced a bit at the word, remembering how stressed James was as he fought to keep his son from a prison sentence. "It's hardly a prison, Kelly."

Kelly glanced over with raised eyebrows. "If you say so—but you sure don't have a whole lot of freedom. Not all prisons have bars on the windows, you know."

"Can we enjoy the afternoon without your preaching today?"

"Only because I love you. We'll call a truce, and I'll even buy you a lobster roll for dinner later on – wherever you want."

Arlene smiled, grateful for the woman who'd become a good friend over the years. She'd never been able to keep a friend until she met the brunch club. Her father had been a drunk and too embarrassing to have friends over, and the girls she met in secretarial school all snubbed her when James came along and insisted she quit. Most of the classmates she hung out with had left Gloucester, determined to find a life away from fishing boats and factory jobs. James offered her an escape from the same fate, promising a stable and comfortable life as the wife of a young lawyer.

"Hey, where'd your mind drift off to?"

"I was actually thinking about how grateful I am that James chose you as our realtor; we might never have become friends."

"It helped when I noticed a skein of yarn sticking out of your bag the first time, I showed you a house. I'm glad, too. You've been a good friend, especially during the last couple of years."

"I'm still praying that the two of you will reconcile someday. I'd hate you to throw away a good marriage over one simple mistake."

"I'd hardly call sleeping with my college roommate a simple mistake."

"Even if it was Angie's fault?"

"It takes two," Kelly snarled.

"But he'd been drinking, and that—"

"Look, can we not spoil the day? I know how you feel about Travis and me, but I'm not ready to consider trying again. I can't be with someone I don't trust."

Arlene's tone softened. "But you haven't divorced him, either – so you must still love him."

Kelly's eyes got a little misty as her jaw stiffened. "Love isn't always enough. Not when the trust is gone." She exhaled slowly. "Now can we table this discussion and focus on something more important—like yarn?"

The brightly colored sign came into view, and Arlene smiled. "Agreed. Nothing like a wall display of yarn to take your troubles away.

At least for a little while." She smiled at Kelly as she reached for her purse. "Thanks for calling today. I think we can both use a little escape."

"Damn right. And while I suspect you're buying those blue and orange skeins you admired last time, promise me you'll take your time and peruse every single option beforehand."

"I'd be happy to do that for you. What are friends for?"

"Let's go touch a bunch of soft stuff. God, I love yarn therapy."

"Look at you, giving thanks to God," Arlene teased as they climbed the steps.

"Don't start with that crap, girlfriend. I haven't stepped inside a church since high school and I don't plan to start any time soon."

"I'm still gonna pray for you." She reached out and opened the door, gesturing for Kelly to lead the way. "Now let's go play."

CHAPTER FIVE

Kim McBride was relieved. *The banners are coming down; thank God Fiesta is over for another year.* She headed out of town as all the tourists jammed the roads leading in, and avoided the harbor area in general when she could. The one exception she made was for coffee, as the Brine and Brew served the best coffee in town. *A quick in and out – which is the way I like—*

"Morning, sunshine." A familiar voice interrupted her thoughts and smashed any chance of a quick exit. She turned with a forced smile to face the one man she'd hoped to avoid.

"Hey. Shouldn't you be way off shore by now?"

Bill smiled, revealing the dimple on his right cheek. "Nate had a doctor's appointment. Working over in the sail shop today instead – way better hours, I might add."

"I hear congratulations are in order."

Bill paused before replying. "Wasn't sure you'd heard – but yeah, I snagged it as I fell."

"I'm sure everyone enjoyed the celebration. So, what's up with Nate? He never takes a day off."

"He can't refill his blood pressure medicine without an appointment."

"Poor Terri. No doubt he's grumpier than hell this morning."

"I feel bad for the doc – he's gonna get an earful, making him come in ."

As they to the front of the line Kim put her order in and gave the barista a twenty. "I'll take care of his, too – gotta treat the champ."

The young guy's face lit up. "Hey, you're the Greasy Pole winner! Viva!" Both locals and tourists alike joined in the cheer, lifting their coffee to toast Bill. "Viva!" The young man waved them past. "On the house – both of you. Next!"

Shit. This is just what I didn't need. Kim tried to protest as the guy handed her back the money, but then sheepishly folded the bill and put it in her pocket. "Can't say I didn't try to treat. You must be getting a lot of that this week."

Bill grinned. "It'll pass; next week a new crowd of tourists will be here and I'll just be Bill the fisherman again. But thanks for the gesture." They stood awkwardly silent for a moment before he continued. "It was tough standing up by the winner's board, not gonna lie."

Kim blinked back tears, knowing she had to reply. "I'm sure he was proud of you."

"Kind of all came crashing back. I didn't expect that."

"Which explains why I avoid the whole weekend." The ache inside grew stronger, and luckily Kim spotted their coffee being placed on the counter. "That's ours."

Bill reached out and grabbed both, handing one to Kim slowly. "Ya know, you *could* still treat me to coffee another time. Maybe tonight?"

"I can't; there's an organ concert at the castle and I'm working late. I guess I'll see you around."

Bill held onto the outside of her hand for a moment, forcing her to meet his gaze. "It *does* get easier, Sunshine. I promise."

Kim tried to find solace in his smile, but only saw the face of Anthony as she pulled her hand away. "Does it?" She wiped her eyes with her free hand and walked past him. "Congrats again. And tell Nate I said hi."

He waited for her to leave, then sipped his coffee as he crossed the street at the Fishermen's Monument, where the guilt washed over him as he read the words etched in the stone. *They that go down in ships...* Blinking back his own tears, he looked out past the breakwater to the open sea. *I tried so hard to save you, Bud. You should still be here – for her. The girl we both fell in love with.* Only the gulls answered.

    * * *

On the other side of the harbor Kim eventually pulled into the parking lot at Hammond Castle and hurried inside. "Sorry I'm late; still lots of traffic coming through town."

Jacqueline Palmer, the Director of the Museum, smiled from behind the counter of the gift shop as she prepared the daily till. "No problem. And thank you for staying late tonight to close up. I'd much rather be here for the organ concert than sitting at some investors meeting.

Kim laughed as she passed by. "Yeah, but those investors help to keep this place open – and pay our salaries. I'll see you later. I want to turn all the lights on before the first tour is set to go!" She made her way through the Great Hall and the courtyard, glad to reach the exhibit rooms. She much preferred talking about Medieval weaponry than explaining how the other spots were perfect places for weddings. *For other people – but not for me.*

As she finished her tour set up her thoughts wandered to her earliest memory of the castle when she fell in love with it on a class field trip. She told her teacher on the bus ride back to school that someday she'd work and be married here. The teacher smiled, answering with a sweet "How nice, dear."

But here she was. She started working in the gift shop when she turned sixteen and never left. Throughout college years she worked weekends and every break, and even after starting a full-time teaching job she remained on staff for summer employment and special events. Like weddings. She couldn't count all the weddings she had coordinated before planning her own. The one that never happened.

Alright, Kim, pull yourself together. Fiesta is over and you have five tours and an organ concert to manage today. Hours later, she sat in the Great Hall and lost herself in the music. Her mom had instilled in her a love of the classics, and the Hammond organ was the perfect channel for the Baroque masterpieces being performed this evening. The soloist, Professor Edward Pennington from Merrimack College, had offered many concerts over the years and played the organ like a friend who knew it intimately.

Kim closed her eyes, letting Bach's fugues wash away her pain. By the time the last guest had gone and only Edward and the security guard remained, Kim felt more peaceful.

"Another beautiful concert, Edward. I think the entire audience was mesmerized."

The attractive musician loosened the tie of his tuxedo. "And what about you, my lovely? Was I able to mesmerize you as well?"

She smiled at the dark eyes and neatly combed hair. "It was exactly what I needed to raise my spirits tonight."

"And need I ask what caused the maiden's melancholic mood?"

She allowed him to hold open the arched door to the outside as the security guard stayed behind to set the alarm. "Fiesta weekend; still brings back too many memories."

"Ah, yes. I'm so fortunate to live far enough away to only catch glimpses on the evening news. That Greasy Pole vulgarity is nauseating. St. Peter must recoil in his grave."

"Don't be so harsh. All of those fishermen have deep reverence for their patron saint. Fiesta is simply their time to celebrate and let loose a little."

Edward raised his eyebrows with disapproval. "I realize you grew up with the custom, but it's way beneath your level of sophistication. I'll choose the music of the masters over the drunken sea shanties any day."

"You did make the masters proud tonight – the Bach fugue especially."

He gently reached for her hand as he held her gaze. "One of these days you're finally going to agree to go out with me."

Kim blushed. Edward had been interested for well over a year, proving to be both patient and persistent. She gave his hand a squeeze before releasing it. "Perhaps. But not today. Good night, Edward. Thank you for the music."

"Good night, my lovely. Until the next time."

CHAPTER SIX

Betty Sue pulled into the driveway of her mom's house as her phone rang. Seeing the familiar name appear on the screen improved her mood temporarily. "Well, hi there."

"How's my Southern Belle doing on this fine afternoon?"

He could make her smile so easily. "Looking forward to our dinner date more than I can say."

"That's funny; I'm looking much more forward to the dessert later on."

She blushed, feeling more alive than she had in years. "I love when you talk naughty."

"Oh, I plan on doing a lot more than talking naughty, sugar."

Betty Sue could feel her desire growing. "I'll hold you to that. I may be a little bit late picking you up; I need to deal with Mother first."

"Where's that kid of yours? I thought she did the night shift."

"She'll be along shortly. I'll call you when I'm leaving—and I'll make it up to you later."

"Hmm-mmm. You grab yourself a little snack while getting Elena settled. I might insist on dessert *before* dinner. I'll be waiting, sugar."

Betty Sue tucked her phone away and let the air conditioning cool her flushed cheeks. *Carla better not be late; I haven't been this horny in years.*

She unlocked the front door and called out. "Mother! It's Betty Sue." The toilet flushed down the hallway as she stopped to click off the blaring game show on television. As she entered the kitchen, her nose wrinkled at the smell of fish. *Oh, dear Lord. What has she done now?* She followed the scent to discover an open container of tuna fish in the dish cabinet. Swatting away a fly, she closed the lid and dropped it in the trash, and then opened a window as she turned on the exhaust fan. *She's such a pain in the butt.*

Elena greeted her in a housecoat and socks. "Hello, dear. I thought that was your voice."

"Where are your slippers? Those socks don't give you enough traction on the floors."

"I guess I misplaced them. Maybe they're under the bed. There's tuna in the fridge if you're hungry. I picked some up yesterday on the way home."

"No, Mother," Betty Sue said gently, trying to hide the strain in her voice. "*I* brought you the tuna fish on *Saturday*—five days ago! It wasn't in the fridge. You put it in the cupboard instead − couldn't you smell it?"

Oblivious, Elena sniffed her housecoat. "My clothes always do after work. Hard to get that fish scent out sometimes. How are you dear?"

Betty Sue sighed. "I'm okay, Mother. I brought you dinner since Carla is working late again." She started taking containers out of her bag. "I made pasta e fagioli this afternoon."

Elena's face brightened as she eagerly approached the table. "My favorite! Did you bring fresh bread, too?"

Her daughter pulled out a small loaf of Italian bread. "Of course I did." *I buy a loaf at the market and throw away the bag. Fools you every time.*

The older woman held it in her hands and sniffed slowly. "Hmm... you make the best bread." She patted her daughter's face. "I'm glad you're home, dear. We can all eat together when Carla gets back."

"Why don't we have some now? She can heat it up. Go on, sit down."

She grabbed one bowl and one smaller bread plate and served her mom the pasta and bean dish with a slice of bread. Remembering her earlier phone call, she grinned and grabbed a second small plate. *He did tell me to grab a snack, after all.*

"Would you like something to drink?" She opened the refrigerator to see what was on hand and stopped short. Elena's slippers were on the top shelf straddling a bowl of grapes.

"Mother, your slippers are in the *fridge.*"

Elena glanced over with a perplexed look on her face. "Now how did they end up there? I know I put them in the closet." She picked up her spoon nonchalantly. "Now come eat while it's hot."

Sighing, Betty Sue joined her at the table and cut two slices of bread, spreading each with butter before placing one on the small dish next to Elena's soup bowl. She took a bite of the other slice and smiled, her thoughts once again anticipating the evening ahead.

"You look radiant tonight," Elena said between slurps. "Must be the new man you keep yakking about."

And just like that your mind can be clear as a bell. God, I hate dementia. "As a matter of fact, I'm going to bring him to your birthday party in a couple of weeks, and he can't wait to meet you." *And I can't wait to meet him later on. Where the hell is Carla?*

"My birthday? Are you making me a cake?"

"Jean will bring the cake. Your favorite."

"So, what does Jean think of the new beau?"

"She hasn't met him yet—but I'm having the girls over for brunch the Saturday before to meet him. And then I'll bring him here that Sunday when I come."

"Are we having a party?"

"Jean and Hannah will be here. And Carla, of course."

"My sweet Carla. Takes such good care of me."

Betty Sue felt a twinge of resentment. *You never tell me that I take good care of you. Only Carla. Sometimes I wonder why I moved back from Tennessee.*

"She should be home soon. Said she was only staying an extra hour."

"And then you'll leave again. You always do." Elena sopped up the thick stew with her bread as Betty Sue's resentment grew again. Her mother had a knack of sneaking in her judgmental phrases in such a casual manner. Many thought she did so perfectly innocently, but Betty Sue was sure of her intent each time.

"I *do* own my own home, Mother. But I'm always a phone call away – you know that." Carla's old car sputtering into the driveway brought a smile back onto her face. "Sounds like that daughter of mine is finally here. I'll put these other containers in the fridge for you before I leave."

"Hey, Nonna, I'm home," Carla announced as she entered. She dumped her backpack on the chair closest to the door and carried a paper bag into the kitchen. "Hi, mom," she said, before kissing her grandmother on the cheek. "Pasta e fagioli? You must be feeling guilty to bring her favorite."

"Try some, my dear," Elena said, gesturing to the container Betty Sue had left on the counter. "It's delicious, and she baked fresh bread, too."

Carla chuckled as she glared across the table. "Yeah, sure she did. I grabbed a meatball sub to bring home. Would you like a piece, Nonna?"

Elena shook her head. "This is more than enough. Ask your mother, though."

Betty Sue pushed her chair back. "Actually, now that Carla's home, I need to be on my way."

"Another hot and heavy date tonight?" Carla sneered.

"As a matter of fact, yes. I'm picking him up for dinner, and I'm running late because you weren't home on time."

Carla slammed her plate down on the table. "Well pardon me for having a *job* while you fart around town all day. I'd love *one* night off every now and then to go out after working my butt off all day." She plopped down on her chair, lowering her volume as she glared at her mother. "Instead, I'm stuck here babysitting every night!"

"Ooh, is that a meatball sub?" Elena asked. "I might like a little bit of that." Carla sighed as her tone softened. "Sure, Nonna, let me cut a little section off for you."

For a moment Betty Sue considered staying to try and offer support, knowing the minutes of clarity in her mother's mind had once again passed. A text, however, changed her mind, and she said her goodbyes and scooted out the door. As she started the car, she read it again and laughed as her desire returned. *"I just bought a can of whipped cream, sugar. Gonna taste great on my dessert."*

After fifteen years of being widowed, Betty Sue had a lot of time to make up for. It would be a naughty night, indeed.

CHAPTER SEVEN

Two weeks later, Sharon Collins' stomach growled as she sat in traffic on the highway thinking about the brunch she was missing. *I forgot Kelly told me to use the last exit to avoid all this congestion. Damn it! I wish I'd grabbed a biscuit for the road.* She'd declined an earlier breakfast at home with her son Tim's famous cheddar biscuits.

She smiled, remembering the banter that flew around the kitchen. Tim's wife Maggie had reunited Sharon and her dad after many estranged years, and every one of them was grateful. Despite the normal aggravations of living together, they made it work and loved every day together.

Still, I love breathing the salt air, and truly enjoy having new friends my own age. As traffic began moving again, she sent a quick text to Betty Sue saying she'd be there soon. *Hopefully in time to meet her new boyfriend. And to finally eat something.*

When she pulled into her parking spot at Tim's townhouse, she left her overnight bag in the car and headed straight next door. She could hear laughter and animated conversation through the open windows, and her pace quickened up the walkway to join in the festivities. Betty Sue opened the door and hugged her tightly. "You *made* it! I'm so glad!" She held her arm as they strolled toward the living room. "There's still plenty to eat, but first, you need to meet my man! The others all love him!"

Sharon waved to the others as Betty Sue walked up behind a chair and leaned over to kiss the graying hair of the man seated. "Sweetie, come and meet my newest friend." As she pulled on his arm, he stood up and turned to face her.

Sharon stood in shock as Betty Sue approached with her arm wrapped around his waist. "Sharon, I want you to meet the new love of my life. This is Sean McClean. Sean, Sharon Collins."

It can't be. Not him. Oh, my God, not him. In a frozen moment, all the memories of Sean McClean ruining her life came flooding back in a tsunami. Having lost the ability to speak or react, she almost recoiled as Sean reached out his hand. "Sharon Collins, I have *so* looked forward to finally meeting you. Betty Sue has told me so much about your weekend trips up to the shore."

Sharon felt almost dizzy. *How can you stand there and pretend we're strangers?* Her stomach growled and she was afraid she might hurl on the rug, but before she could move Sean spoke again, this time to the whole group. "Now ladies, much as I have *loved* this warm reception, I unfortunately need to leave for a meeting. No rest for the wicked. It was a pleasure – and if you don't mind, I'm gonna steal this little ray of sunshine for a quick private goodbye outside."

Betty Sue patted his stomach and smiled. "Let me grab your bag and I'll walk you out, sweetie."

Sharon didn't move. Her mind raced, but was unable to process anything. Sean glanced around the room to make sure no one was watching before speaking. His whisper was dripping with satisfaction. "Darlin', seeing you speechless has made my day. And for now, we're gonna keep our past a little secret, understand? You missed your moment."

Say something, damn it! Scream! Tell them all how vile you are! Sharon opened her mouth, but the words were frozen in her mind. As Betty Sue returned to earshot distance, Sean's volume increased and tone brightened. "And I'm so glad you arrived in time to finally meet." He reached out and wrapped his arm protectively around Betty Sue's waist, giving her a squeeze. "I can see why she speaks so highly of all of you. Have a wonderful day, ladies! And Sharon, next time we'll get better acquainted."

Betty Sue reached out to pat her arm. "I'll be back in a flash. Go help yourself to some food; should still all be warm."

As she watched them walk out the door, Sean glanced back over his shoulder and grinned at her.

Sharon needed air. *I can't face the brunch club right now.* She walked toward the patio doors, past a table laden with chafing dishes, pastries, croissants, and a fruit tray. The aromas increased the nausea in the pit of her stomach, and she slipped out onto the deck where she leaned against the railing to catch her breath. She blinked back tears, determined to hold it together until she could be alone next door.

Kelly had followed her out. "You okay?"

Sharon quickly wiped her eyes and nodded, still facing the harbor. "I'm fine. My stomach's a little off today—from sitting in traffic, I'm sure." She turned to face Kelly who was now leaning beside her with her back to the railing.

"You, lady, are a lousy liar," Kelly said. "I'm a little more observant than the others. You wanna tell me what the hell just happened in there? I suggest the short version, before she comes back inside."

Sharon exhaled as her shoulders fell. The tension was still pulsing through her body as she replied. "I...I *know* him—all too well. And I wish to God I didn't."

"So, I assume he faked that whole introduction in there?"

Sharon glanced inside to make sure the others were all still engrossed in conversation. She leaned closer to Kelly and spoke in almost a whisper. "Everything about him is an act. He's a lying, manipulative, narcissistic *ass,* and I—"

"Shh! Betty's coming back in. I'll keep them distracted while you get your shit together. But we have a date later for you to fill me in. Got it?"

Sharon nodded as Kelly joined the others. *Of all the people in the world, why him?* And the fact that he was intimately involved with her Gloucester neighbor made her stomach churn. *Kelly's right; I need to eat a little to keep the acid down, and I can't tell Betty Sue anything until I figure out why the hell he's here.* She pasted a smile on her face and stepped back inside, picking up a plate and reaching for a croissant.

Betty Sue's voice spoke above the others. "Soo...what did y'all think? Isn't he a dream?"

Sharon stood back, catching Kelly's reassuring look as the ladies replied.

"Seemed nice enough," Terri offered in her gruff, matter-of-fact manner.

Jean nodded. "Maybe a little forced. Tell him he doesn't have to try so hard to make an impression next time. We're your friends, after all."

Arlene smiled at her hostess. "Well, I thought he was *perfect* gentleman, doting on you all morning. You've been blessed."

Sharon almost choked on her croissant as Betty Sue turned to her. "What about you? What'd you think?"

Kelly stepped in to save her. "Hell, she was only here a minute before he ran off – give her a break. As for me, I can only say to be careful. You haven't known him that long, and I'd never want you to get hurt."

Peg raised her glass. "Go, Kelly, for being the cynic!" She swallowed the last of her bloody mary and put it down in front of her. "Just watch yourself, Betty. He's a man, after all – most of 'em are out to screw ya, literally *and* figuratively. I've had too many of those."

"Men, or bloody marys?" Jean teased.

Peg's laugh was even deeper than Jean's. "Most definitely both."

As conversation veered away from Sean, Sharon was able to sit quietly and nibble on her croissant as her mind continued to race. She caught Kelly's gaze from across the room, wondering how in the world she'd make her friend understand how destructive Sean McClean was. *One thing's for sure. He's not here by accident. He never is.*

CHAPTER EIGHT

With brunch winding down, Sharon desperately wanted to make an exit, and Kelly was ready. "Sharon, didn't you say your son was an architect? Do you think I could walk next door with you and pick your brain a little, maybe have you jot down a few things to ask him? I have a client who's ready to buy, but needs to consult with an architect on some requested updates."

Sharon understood exactly what she was doing, and nodded. "Sure, if Betty Sue doesn't mind us both leaving. It *is* her party, after all."

Betty Sue smiled. "Don't you worry your pretty little head about that. Everyone will be leaving shortly, so feel free to scoot off. I have to pack up the leftovers for Mother's birthday tomorrow."

"Give Elena my best, will you?" Kelly said. "And we'll get together this week sometime."

"Absolutely—and I'll tell you all about the party. I'm a little nervous, as Sean's gonna meet the family."

Sharon wanted to grab her and shake her. *Not the family. Don't let him near your family.* Instead, she thanked her for brunch and gave her a little hug, said goodbye to the others, and walked next door with Kelly beside her. Once inside the townhouse, the emotions let loose and the tears began.

Kelly handed her a box of tissues and gestured toward the couch. "Sit. You need to let a little out before talking." She picked up a remote and turned on the television, pushing buttons to bring up a music station. When Sharon looked at her quizzically, she gestured toward the wall. "Not sure how thin they are, and you don't need Betty Sue running over to check up on you. You got any alcohol in this place?"

Sharon grabbed a few tissues, gesturing toward the kitchen. "Last cabinet on the right," she said between sobs, "but I'm...not a drinker."

Karen returned shortly and handed her a glass of scotch. "You are today, lady. Besides, I don't like to drink alone." She settled down on the couch, leaning one arm on the back cushion and pulling her feet up under her. "Go on – one swig."

Sharon took a gulp, sputtering as the alcohol burned all the way down her throat. "Jesus! You trying to kill me?" The shock stopped the tears, however, and she placed the glass on the table and turned to face a grinning Kelly.

"A little scotch does wonders, doesn't it? So, tell me about this lying, manipulative, narcissistic ass. How long have you known him?"

"We grew up together – went to high school together, and I worked with him in his father's hardware store. Hell, I went to senior prom with him."

"O-kaay...now you have my interest," Karen said, swallowing more scotch. "Didn't realize this went all the way back to childhood, so give me the abridged version first. Then fill in the details."

"He always thought Sean would grow up and take over the family business, but Sean was a party boy who didn't want to work at anything. He was a charmer, though, and we dated until I started seeing him for who he really was."

"We'll come back to that. Move along."

"We went to college together, although I lived at home and took the train while he lived on campus in Boston. He told his parents he wanted the whole university experience, but all he wanted was to party his ass off!" Sharon grimaced as more scotch burned her throat. "He introduced me to his roommate, though, and he seemed different."

"Don't tell me – you ended up marrying the roommate, didn't you?"

Sharon nodded. "His name was Steve Collins, and he was...so *romantic* at first. He could have made something of himself...if it wasn't for Sean McClean. They became business partners right after we got married, and started staying out late all the time—*business* meetings, Steve said. He came home drunk most of the time, and he wasn't as nice anymore. My dad hated him--told him he wasn't allowed at their house anymore because of how he treated me."

Sharon's eyes filled with tears. "My mom cried...a *lot*. And then I found out I was *pregnant,* and I was...scared...of what he might do. I told my folks – on *Mother's* Day. Isn't that funny?" Sharon laughed, and then cried. "They begged me to stay home, but I wouldn't listen. It was the last time I saw my Mom till she was in a nursing home with dementia. She never even knew she had a grandson..."

Kelly held her when she cried. "I can see why you hate him."

Sharon wiped her tears, the anger returning to propel the story forward. "Hell, that's just chapter one." She raised her glass to take another swig, but caught her reflection in the liquor. "What the fuck am I *doin'*?!" She slammed the glass down on the table, spilling some scotch in the process. "This is what *ruined* Steve, after Sean got him drinking. I'll be damned if he does the same thing to *me!*"

"Let me get you some water," Kelly offered. She removed Sharon's glass and wiped up the spill when she returned. "Time to switch to this, and then you can tell me some more."

Sharon took the glass and guzzled almost half of it before continuing. "Sean's influence on everyone was like a hurricane, leaving nothing but destruction in his wake. It wasn't only Steve. His dad passed away, leaving Sean the store, but instead of selling it, he chose to move away and ignore it totally."

"Including upkeep and taxes and all that?" Kelly asked.

"Believe me, *all* that. He was a deadweight when it came to business. Steve was the one who bailed him out when the fiasco finally caught up to him. After that, their own business began floundering. Steve's drinking got worse, and I needed to get a job to keep a roof over our heads and feed our son."

"That's Tim, right? The one who owns this place?"

Sharon smiled. "He kept me going all those years. The only family I had left."

"Wait a minute," Kelly said confused. "Don't you live with him and your *Dad?*"

"I do—for which I'm grateful every day of my life."

"I sense there's a *but* here..."

"Okay, in a nut-shell, so I don't bore you to death...after Steve died, Tim and I inherited the mess he'd left behind, and discovered Steve owned half of the hardware store as part of the bail-out, which brought Sean back into our lives as we wanted to sell it and get rid of the mess. Instead, Sean came up with this crazy idea to build a driving range and golf pro-shop on the site, saying that Caldwell was full of rich people who loved to golf."

"And Tim agreed?"

"He did. I didn't have the chance to talk him out of it as he was living here while I was still in Maine. Turns out he took the job only because it gave him a chance to go to Caldwell, and maybe meet the grandparents he'd never known." The tears returned as she continued. "He went most of his life never knowing his family – hell, he never got to meet my mom, and all because of Sean."

"He really did screw you over, didn't he?"

"Oh, there's still more, believe me. When my dad found out about Sean's plans for the driving range, he went ballistic. And when he realized that Tim was his new partner, he..." Sharon paused between sobs. "He...had a heart attack...and almost died."

"Holy shit – no wonder you hate him so much." Kelly reached out to rub her shoulder. "But your dad recovered, obviously."

"He did – and in the end, that's what brought our family back together." Sharon smiled, wiping away her tears. "That's the last chapter, and it's a good one—which I'll tell you next time. Let's just say we finally got Sean out of our lives forever – at least I *thought* we had."

"Wait a minute...did Sean know that Tim lived here?"

"Ding, ding – I think you've connected the dots. My question is why the hell he's back, and what the hell does he want?"

"And in the meantime, he's dragged Betty Sue into the whole thing." Kelly finished her drink and sat back. "Shit."

"He destroys anything in his path – he always has. He'll do the same with Betty Sue if we don't do something about it. *That* I'm sure about."

"I still can't figure what he wants with Tim – or you, for that matter."

"My best guess is money – when I moved back home, the sale of the house in Maine gave us enough to buy him out of the partnership and pay off all the debts. I suspect he's running out of cash at this point. Maybe that's what brought him here – thinking he could hook into the townhouse somehow."

Kelly's concern grew. "That might be what brought him, but I'm afraid he's moved on to plan B with your neighbor."

"Huh?"

"Don't you get it? Betty Sue's husband left her millions when he died. That's why her life is one big social party."

"And she's as gullible as they come." The reality stung even more than the alcohol. "He doesn't care about me or this townhouse anymore – he's after *her* money now. And he'll screw her over big time – I guarantee it."

"The hell he will," Kelly replied. "Operation Sean Be Gone is now officially underway, and with the others' help, we're gonna save our friend from that asshole."

CHAPTER NINE

Jean and Hannah McBride walked across the street for Elena's party the next day, stopping to enjoy the sea breezes that swirled their way up the hill from the harbor.

"I'll never tire of salty air," Hannah said, breathing deep. "And while the tourists will drive me crazy for the next couple of months, I can't imagine living anywhere else but right here."

Jean nodded, carrying the cake container. "I'm glad; I kinda like having my daughters at home, at least for now."

"So do you think Elena will like Betty Sue's new boyfriend?"

"He's pleasant enough, and I suspect quite the charmer when he wants to be. I'm sure she'll love him. Carla? Not so sure."

"Why wouldn't she like him?"

"Another man whose gonna keep her mom too busy to help with Elena? I predict some stormy weather between those two."

"Hadn't thought of that, but when you put it that way, I'd have to agree with you." They walked around to the back of the house as they always entered through the kitchen. "And in case I never told ya, thanks for not hooking up with a new guy after Dad left. You certainly could have."

Jean laughed. "Honey, one man was *more* than enough for a lifetime.

Besides, I might have ended up with someone even worse. I'll let you get the door; you've got a free hand."

Hannah knocked and called out her greeting as she entered first. "Elena! It's Hannah! And Jean!"

Carla was in the kitchen finishing up some dishes. "Come on in. The birthday girl is in watching the Sox game. My mom and her boyfriend are on their way." As Jean placed the cake on the counter, she continued. "Thanks for making Nonna's favorite."

"Happy to do it," Jean replied. "I'll go in and say hello unless you need me to help with anything."

"Nope, keeping it simple – made a batch of lasagna this morning and mom's bringing leftovers from her brunch. Might be some weird combinations, but what the hell? Nonna won't care."

As Jean headed for the living room, Carla reached for the towel by the sink. "Listen, I need to ask you a *huge* favor for some time this week."

Hannah helped herself to a couple of grapes sitting in a fruit bowl. "If I can; what's up?"

"I hate asking since you're with Nonna all day, but do you think some night soon you could bring her home and stay over? That is, if my mom can't—I'll ask her first."

"Ahh, didn't you just ask me first?" Hannah teased.

"You know what I mean – I don't wanna leave her alone all night. You'd be my back up choice."

"I'm sure I can. God knows you can use a break from time to time. You working extra shifts?"

Carla's face brightened. "Actually, I'm hoping to take a day off at some point and party hard the night before. Been *way* too long...and you'll never guess who's back in town!"

So, she's finally seen him out and about. Figured it was coming.

"JJ Winston-- saw him driving down Stacey Boulevard on his bike, and *man,* he's hotter than ever! I wanna give him a warm welcome home if you get my drift."

Hannah flinched a bit, wondering if JJ would welcome the

advances. "He may not be partying these days – I suspect he's not allowed out all that much."

Carla grinned. "Hey, I can show him a good time without ever stepping inside a bar; and I've made enough in tips the last few weeks to cover a night at Cape Ann Motor Inn. A romantic stroll on the beach at night, followed by—need I elaborate?"

"Sounds like you have it all planned out." *I wonder if JJ will be interested.*

"Hey, it's been, like, forever since I've had a night off, and man, did he put me in the mood when he zoomed past. Once I find out what night works best for him, I'll let you know."

"*After* you ask your mom."

"Duh! I said I would." The sound of voices and car doors being closed drifted through the open windows. "Sounds like the love birds are here," Carla said. "Did you meet him yet?"

Hannah shook her head. "Mom did yesterday. Said he was friendly – almost a little forced, but he was probably nervous meeting the gang. You gonna behave?"

"Do I ever?"

"Give him a chance—your mother sure is smiling these days."

"Only 'cause she's got a man back in her pants again. Not fair she's gettin' more than I am."

"Jeez, you talk like a sailor."

Carla smirked. "I've sure screwed a few...come on, let's go check this guy out."

Betty Sue led Sean across the room. "Mother, this is the wonderful man I've been telling you all about. Sean, my mother Elena."

He lifted Elena's hand and kissed it. "Now I see where your gorgeous daughter gets her looks. I'm so pleased to meet you – especially on your birthday. I picked these up just for you." He handed her a small bouquet, and Elena accepted them with a smile.

"How lovely! I love flowers! I need to find a vase."

"I'll do that, Mother – and then I'll bring this handsome man back to visit some more." She pulled Sean by the arm. "Sweetie, this is my daughter Carla and Jean's daughter, Hannah. Girls, this is Sean."

Carla nodded without extended her hand. "Hey. "

Sean grinned. "Your mom's told me plenty of wonderful things about you."

"Yeah, sure she has," Carla retorted.

If Sean picked up on the sarcasm, he hid it well. "I guess that makes you Hannah."

"I'm Carla's best friend," Hannah added. "Nice to meet you after hearing Betty Sue's glowing reports."

Sean's face lit up as he wrapped his arm around Betty Sue's shoulder. "I guess you *have* been talking about me, huh? Hope it didn't include *all* the good stuff, sugar."

"Oh, you," she cooed, patting his belly. "A lady never tells those kinds of secrets. Should we bring in the rest of the food?"

Carla held up her hand. "Hannah and I will take care of it – you visit with Nonna. Is the car open?"

Sean nodded. "Yep. Bags on the back seat. Thanks, Carla. It's mighty fine of you to offer." Not waiting for a response, he spun Betty Sue around and gave her a squeeze before approaching the couch next to Elena's chair.

Carla waited until she was outside before reacting. "Gee, *thanks* Carla. It's *mighty fine* of you to offer," she mocked. "What the hell was *that*?"

"Okay, so he loses points for trying a little too hard."

"Ya think?"

"But he did bring Elena flowers."

"Big deal. They were from the $4.99 clearance bucket at the market."

"I take it you're not impressed?"

"Hell, it don't matter. My opinion doesn't count for shit in her book, which is fine with me. I learned how to fend for myself a long time ago."

"She at least moved back home."

Carla spun around like a spitfire. "The *hell* she did! She bought a damn townhouse near the beach, and goes around telling everyone how she came home to take care of her mother, when *I'm* the one who's here dealing with all the crap! We haven't gotten a single *dime* of her money to help out. She doesn't give a shit about me *or* Nonna."

"So, why would she have left Tennessee? I think you need to cut her a little slack sometimes."

Carla slammed the car door. "Thanks, but I did that when I was seven years old—right after she left me for a guy who didn't want someone else's kid to raise. Not exactly mother-of-the-year material."

"Maybe she wants a chance to start over."

"Jesus, Hannah, your damn counseling doesn't cut it, okay? Ask *her* why she's back. It sure as hell ain't guilt. As for me, as soon as Nonna's gone, I'm out of this crappy town forever."

Hannah followed her back into the house at a distance. *Man, she's wound up tight − God help us if she lets loose in there. Might be one hell of a birthday party.*

CHAPTER TEN

Kim arrived at Hammond Castle early for her meeting with Jacqueline, and stopped outside to admire the Gothic arches overlooking the harbor. Even with the summer heat increasing, there was almost always a shore breeze in this shaded courtyard just outside the Great Room. She sat on the base, leaning against one of the arches, and breathed in the salt air as she sipped her iced coffee. The sound of waves lapped gently on the rocks below as the tide ebbed.

The coffee brought back her chance encounter with Bill at the coffee shop, and she sighed, remembering countless days spent with him and Anthony growing up. After years of admiring Bill with no response, Anthony's drunken kiss after his greasy pole victory sealed her fate. Months later, when they got engaged, Bill agreed to be Anthony's best man. *So why is it so hard to still run into him now? Maybe we're both missing our best friend, that's all.*

Letting the salt air blow the thoughts away, she walked briskly through the Great Room and found Jacqueline in her office sipping tea as she waited. "Sorry I'm late; got distracted this morning."

"I saw you out the window and figured you'd be in soon. Glad to see you perched out there; you've avoided that area for quite some time."

"Yeah; but today was more peaceful."

"Well, that might make this meeting go a little more smoothly."

Kim made herself comfortable. "How so?"

"Last night I accepted a board nomination for the New England Museum Association."

Kim's face lit up. "That's awesome! You've waited a long time."

Her boss smiled. "True, and I have to admit I'm pretty excited about it. However, it *is* going to necessitate some changes here." Jacqueline slid a packet across the desk, and Kim flinched, recognizing the color-coded pink folders. "I've covered the weddings for as long as I could, but I need to pass them back to you."

"But...you were going to let Dorothy handle them."

"There's no time to train her at this point. You're ready for them again, I'm sure of it."

Kim reluctantly picked up the packet and opened the first folder. *This one's only a few weeks away – I'll never be ready.*

"I know it's soon, but it's only three hours with fifty people, and the contract's been reviewed and signed. Only thing you'll need to do is talk to Vinny – he's down for photographs."

Kim sighed. *Vinny. Of course, it would be Vinny.* "Jacqueline, I'm not sure—"

"Look, I know he's Anthony's brother, but he's a friend of the bride. His new number is on the form. He's living with Peg Fernandez right now."

"Yeah, I'm glad he's got a safe place to live. Peg's like family."

"His parents haven't budged?"

"Sadly, no. But Anthony died right after he'd come out, and I guess it was easier to ignore their gay kid while grieving the other."

"But Vinny's their only living son."

"Tell that to God. First, he takes their older child, and then tells them their younger kid is going to hell. I'm a little pissed off at the Church in case you hadn't noticed."

"Understandable. And much as I'd love to keep chatting, you have a group due in twenty minutes and I have some budget stuff to work on." She gestured toward Kim's packet of pink wedding folders. "I know you'll be fine with those."

Kim shrugged. "That makes one of us."

* * *

Later that day, Vinny Rossi stopped in to review his part of the wedding contract. They sat at a table in the circular library which overlooked the harbor. *He looks so much like his brother, and yet couldn't be more different.* "How are you holding up these days?"

"I take each day as it comes. Helps to minimize the hurt."

"I totally get it – kinda dreading the weddings again."

"Hey, Sarah's a close friend, and I promise this one will be low-key. Besides, I'll be around if you need a hug."

"I'll keep that in mind," Kim replied. "Here's our standard list of rooms; give me a list of what parts of the castle need to be open for photos after you meet with her."

"Easy enough; I'm having her and Keith over to Peg's for dinner this weekend to finalize everything."

"How's Peg these days?"

"She's awesome. I lucked out getting one of her rooms – complete with therapy cats."

"Ah, yes, the crazy cat lady – what's the count up to these days?"

"Nine--five black and four orange tabbies. Halloween colors, she said."

"Jeez...I go crazy with two." Kim looked up at the clock and closed her file. "I won't keep you; thanks for coming by."

Vinny nodded as he stood up, pausing awkwardly. "I'm sorry I never got you as a sister-in-law. You and Anthony were good together."

Kim blinked back the tears, determined not to let her emotions win out. "Thanks; we really were."

"I must admit, I always thought you and Bill would end up together. Then all of a sudden, you were with Anthony. Go figure."

What's with me and Bill? Why does everyone keep saying that? "Hey, don't be a stranger, okay?"

Vinny grinned. "I won't. And if it helps, I have the other weddings coming up as well, and I'll help you get through them." He picked up the form he needed and tucked it into his notebook. "See ya round."

As she watched him leave, she looked out at the incoming tide. Dark clouds on the horizon promised rain and possible thunderstorms later in the evening. *Weddings at the castle again. Talk about stormy weather indeed.*

CHAPTER ELEVEN

By the time August rolled around, the summer heat had climbed along with the influx of tourists, and while the restaurants loved the business, the locals hated the traffic. Sharon Collins cursed as she made her way past the Fishermen's Monument toward Kelly's condo. The latter had convinced Sharon to stay with her for the weekend so they could reveal Sean's past to everyone except Betty Sue. *I hope she knows what she's doing today.*

Traffic lightened as she made her way past the State Fish Pier toward Atlantic Rd, and soon she was pulling in to Kelly's condo, situated directly across the street from the pounding surf on Bass Rocks. *Man, her ocean views are even better than Tim's.*

A yappy bark greeted her as she rang the bell, and Kelly met her at the door with a white ball of fluff in her arms. "You made it! This is Chianti – he tries to be ferocious."

Sharon reached out to scratch behind his ears as Chianti licked her hand, his tail wagging furiously. "You're a cutie. And your mom's kitchen smells heavenly."

"Put the chowder on first thing this morning – come on, everyone's here."

Sharon followed her through the kitchen, and up a small flight of steps to the living room, which sat along the ocean side. Terri and Jean sat on the couch, Peg and Arlene on wingback chairs, and Kelly gestured for Sharon to join her on the loveseat on the opposite wall. "You all remember Sharon – except Peg. I don't think you met her yet, did you?"

"Nice to meet you," Sharon said warmly, "And to see the rest of you again. Beautiful home, by the way." She sat down nervously, all of a sudden reluctant to speak out about Betty Sue's new beau.

Arlene spoke up before anyone else could. "I don't understand why Betty Sue wasn't invited – or even *told* about today. Dishonesty is wrong."

Peg offered reassurance. "Kelly said she'd explain, and she must have a reason for the discretion. So, what's up?"

Kelly glanced at Sharon. "You want me to start this off, and then you can fill in the blanks?"

Sharon nodded, apprehensive to open up to women she'd only met a couple of times. *Please let them believe it all, and not react like I'm some outsider causing trouble.* She watched their faces as Kelly filled them in on all she'd shared beforehand, and relaxed when she saw the concern grow.

"So, he's only after her money?" Jean asked incredulously.

"But he *adores* her," Arlene rebuffed. "He treats her like a princess."

Terri shook her head. "Nawh, something about him ain't right. He was trying too hard to impress all of us."

Peg leaned forward in her chair. "Sharon, you're absolutely sure this isn't tied back to you somehow? I mean, why Betty Sue? And how did he end up in Gloucester anyhow?"

Sharon expected her to ask the hard questions, as Kelly had explained her years as a journalist. "He knew my son had bought one of the townhomes, and I'm sure he came around looking for him, not aware that Tim had moved back to Caldwell. Betty Sue did say she first met him in the parking lot and he was asking if Tim still lived in one of the units."

"And Betty Sue," Kelly chimed in, "is such a gullible little social butterfly—I'm sure she told him all about Tim and Sharon."

Peg wasn't convinced. "But if you can rat him out, wouldn't he be more likely to try and avoid you at all costs?"

"Like I told Kelly, he's a narcissistic ass. He's enjoying my involvement – almost taunting me to play."

"Sounds like a piece of crap to me," Terri surmised. "So, what are we supposed to do about it?"

Kelly's eyes brightened. "*We* have to protect Betty Sue's fortune – by working together to take him down."

Silence followed, and Sharon held her breath as each woman assessed the situation.

Arlene spoke first, fiddling with her wedding band. "I think we should leave it alone. She'll fall apart if we interfere."

"But if it's all a façade," Jean pointed out, "the hurt's unavoidable."

"Yeah, better to save her money so she has something left afterwards," Terri added. "Don't be so trusting, Arlene – some people are assholes, and he sounds like one."

"Peg nodded. "The big question is, how the hell are we gonna take this guy down?"

Sharon sighed with relief. "I have no idea. If I confront Betty Sue, she may not believe me – I know how persuasive he can be."

Kelly agreed. "She's right; we can't compete with his midnight whispers. We have to figure out how to make *her* end it by seeing him for who he is – without us actually telling her."

"Easier said than done," Terri said, standing up and rubbing her lower back. "Sorry, gotta stretch this damn sciatica. Your couch is too damn soft for my butt right now."

"Look, ladies," Kelly responded, "this isn't going to be something we figure out right away. We all need to keep our eyes and ears open for anything that might put some doubt in her mind." She glanced at Arlene, who was still playing with her wedding band. "I know it feels a little dishonest, but in the end, we're saving her from being hurt even more."

"I guess. But I don't keep secrets well. What if I screw up and say something? *Then* what happens?"

"If it helps, we'll try to limit your involvement," Terri said. "As for today, you can say you were here for lunch – that's not lying."

"Damn right – about time I fed all of you. I have a platter of assorted wraps and a big pot of chowder in the crock pot. Let's brainstorm over lunch."

* * *

Later that evening Sharon joined her hostess out on her upstairs deck as the waves crashed across the street. Kelly handed her a glass of red wine. "There are lightweight blankets inside that bin if you need them; once the sun goes down the air gets a little chilly."

"Thanks, I'm good for right now. God, I'd never tire of a view like this."

"The unit at the far end is for sale right now if you want to be my neighbor."

Sharon took a sip of wine. "Unfortunately, the chunk of change I got for selling my Maine home ended up going to Sean McClean when my son bought him out."

"You could have bought a nice retirement home with that kind of money. Any regrets?"

Sharon shook her head. "Not at all. It was either my house or Tim's townhouse, and we both wanted to hold on to that. Besides, I love being in Caldwell right now; having my dad back in my life has brought more joy than I ever dreamed of. A lot to be said for reconciliation."

Kelly reached for the bottle to top her glass off. "You trying to call *me* out now?"

"Huh? I was still talking about my dad."

Kelly sat back, putting her feet up on the ottoman and pensively tracing the rim of her wine glass with her finger. "Sorry. The others give me a lot of flak – especially Arlene—and I over-reacted."

"About your separation?"

Kelly sighed. "They all think I'm nuts not to take him back – but I don't feel ready yet. The hurt's still too deep, and the trust isn't there right now. How the hell do I build it back up?"

"Sounds like you do still love him, though."

"Hell, I've loved Travis almost since the first time we met – but love's not always enough when you've been screwed over by two people who mean more than most."

"Look, I'll be the last one to ever judge you. I know what it's like to be separated from the ones you love most – *and* what it's like to be screwed over." She paused a minute, listening to the waves while searching for the right words. "But one thing I *will* say is that when the chasm grows to a certain width and depth, bridging the distance is almost impossible. I'd hate to see you reach that point, that's all."

For a few minutes the only sounds were the waves and an occasional car driving by. Kelly finally broke the silence in almost a whisper. "I couldn't lose him a second time. I'm not nearly as strong as most people think I am."

"Sounds like you don't talk about it much, either."

Kelly glanced over and nodded. "You read people well, you know that? I tried talking to both Betty Sue and Arlene, but neither were helpful. Betty Sue had just moved back and only seemed to want to vent about Elena disrupting her life. And Arlene?"

"Little too heavy on the Biblical advice?"

This time Kelly raised her glass to Sharon. "Here's to all that love and forgiveness crap. Sorry – she has a heart of gold, and I love her dearly. I've even gotten used to having her pray for me. But there are vast differences when it comes to faith, and her advice is faith based."

Sharon took a long sip of wine before speaking. "If you're ever interested, I can promise no advice and no judgement. Just putting it out there."

Kelly shivered a bit. "I'm ready for one of the blankets. Want one?" When Sharon nodded, she retrieved two from the plastic bin, handing one to Sharon before wrapping herself up in the other before sitting back down. So, what do you wanna know?"

Sharon snuggled into the other blanket, suspecting a long tale was ahead. "Whatever you're ready to share. Trust your intuition."

Kelly wrapped the blanket around herself a little tighter, and sipped on her wine. "I love this time of night, when the traffic disappears and all you hear is the sound of the surf."

Sharon accepted Kelly's reluctance to talk and relaxed to the lullaby of the waves. *She's a lot like me, keeping things inside. She'll tell me when the time is right.* Before Kelly ever had a chance, Sharon fell asleep listening to the waves.

* * *

The morning sun woke Sharon, and for a moment she was disoriented. She remembered Kelly waking her up and telling her to go to bed, and then half stumbling in the dark to find the guest bedroom. *Whew! Not sure if it was the wine or the sea air, but man, did I sleep.*

She smiled as she spotted two black beady eyes staring at her from the doorway. "Morning, Chianti," she mumbled, only to have a white furball launch himself onto the bed to give her a friendly kiss. "Well, hey there," she said, scratching behind his ears as he snuggled up next to her. "I should bring you home to meet Tramp one of these days."

A gentle knock on the door announced Kelly's greeting. "Morning. I had left the door open a crack last night; I hope he didn't come in here and bother you during the night."

Chianti barked and wagged his tail as he turned his attention to Kelly. "If he did, I slept right through it," Sharon replied. "What time is it?"

"A little after 8:00; I think we both slept in a bit. I laughed at you last night – you just conked out right in your chair."

Sharon smiled. "I hope you hadn't poured your heart out to me and then realized it was all for naught."

"Nope; I was too relaxed and didn't wanna dredge it all up right before bed; I would have been sitting up all night if I had."

Sharon sat up in bed and stretched. "Makes total sense."

"Today, however, is a new day. In the mood for breakfast and a long story? The Elks Lodge is right down the street, and breakfast is open to the public. You in?"

"For breakfast I don't have to cook? You bet!"

Kelly grinned. "Great. I'll go down and take Chianti out for a quick walk beforehand."

"Sounds like a plan. Meet you downstairs in fifteen minutes."

Thirty minutes later they had walked the short distance to the Gloucester Elks, and Kelly led Sharon upstairs to their primary function room. Glass windows ran along the entire front of the building, with a small raised stage at the back and a parquet dance floor in the middle.

Once seated, a perky young blonde appeared with a smile. "Morning, ladies! My name's Robin, and I'll be taking care of you today. Ready for some coffee?"

Both women nodded, and as Robin went to fetch their caffeine Sharon admired the surf. "Almost enough to make me wanna join the Elks – do you guys ever get tired of the view?"

Kelly grinned. "Haven't yet – although a couple of nor'easters had me wishing my condo was a little further back from the road."

Robin returned with a coffee pot and filled their cups. "Help yourself whenever you're ready, and enjoy your breakfast. Flag me down if you need a refill, 'kay?"

"She's certainly cheerful," Sharon noted as they walked up to the buffet table.

"Robin? Yeah, she's here all the time, either serving or working the kitchen. She must live in the area as we pass each other a lot while out walking." She gestured toward the chafing dishes laden with eggs, potato, bacon, sausage, pancakes, and assorted fruits and baked goods. "What'd I tell ya?"

"Quite the spread. Glad I'm hungry."

As they sat back down to eat, Kelly took a few bites before meeting Sharon's gaze. "So...I was up late last night thinking about what you said – about how the chasm can grow too wide and deep to pass over. I like to think I'm not quite there yet."

"I sense a 'but' coming."

Kelly nodded. "So how do you meet in the middle of a chasm without falling in? It seems unfair to cross over to his side and risk being hurt all over."

"So, invite him to your side, where you still have the control."

Kelly sat cutting her pancake into tiny little pieces before continuing. "If I tell you the story, will you promise not to tell me what to do?"

Sharon smiled. "Lady, it's hard enough keeping myself out of trouble; I don't have the time or energy to tell other people how to manage their messes."

Kelly took a deep breath and exhaled slowly. "I'll try to give the short version...Travis and I met in college our sophomore year, and it really was almost love at first sight. We got married a year after graduation, and were together up until we split two years ago."

"That's a long time to be together."

"Next year should be our thirtieth – and yet I wonder if we'll make it."

"Sounds like you had a solid marriage – so what happened?"

"Angie Landino happened – my college roommate and ex-best friend."

"Now I understand what you meant last night about the two people closest to you. Ouch."

"To put it mildly. Travis had gone to Boston for a marketing conference, and I had a huge closing scheduled and couldn't go. Angie happened to be at the hotel having dinner with a couple other alumni, which led to numerous drinks and a less than innocent nightcap."

Sharon took a sip of her coffee. "Another relationship screwed up by alcohol. And you wonder why I don't drink much?"

"When he got home, I noticed a change. Like he was afraid to look me in the eye, and never wanted to talk about the trip. I tried to let it go, but something inside kept nagging at me."

"He never told you?"

"Not until he had to. At my fiftieth birthday party, one of our friends started talking about the trip, and how Travis was so drunk that Angie offered to help him back to his room."

"Talk about a shitty birthday present."

"Tell me about it. I sat there watching her dote all over him when the cake came out, putting all the pieces together as she lit the candles." Kelly gazed out toward the shore. "I never did blow those candles out—"

"How you ladies doing? Need more coffee?" Robin stood at their table, her smile warm as ever.

Sharon shook her head slightly. "I think we're good," she answered quietly.

Robin glanced over at Kelly and concern replaced the smile. "Hope everything's okay. I'll be back with the check."

"You okay?" Sharon asked as Robin stopped at the next table.

Kelly blinked back tears and sniffled. "I'll be fine. You were right about being a good listener."

"So did you throw the cake at them with candles blazing?"

Kelly almost grinned. "Wish I'd thought of that. I remember people singing, and Travis smiling – don't remember where she was – and as they all clapped, I asked him straight out if he'd been with her that night. His face told me everything—so guilty and so hurt. I walked out of my party without batting an eye."

"That doesn't sound like a man having an affair, though. The guilt, yeah – but not the hurt."

"He swears it was only the one night and he didn't even remember it, but I couldn't even touch him, never mind be his wife. After about a week I asked him to leave, and that's how we've been for over two years now."

"Where did he go?"

"He rents an extended stay room, and lives on the boat during the summer. I have the condo. He has the boat."

Sharon saw a single tear trickling down Kelly's face. "You still miss him?"

"It would be so much easier if I didn't. I've thought of calling him so many times, but never seem capable of hitting that final button on my phone."

Before Sharon could reply, Robin returned with the check. "Here you go, ladies. I hope your day gets better. Life's too short not to enjoy the sunshine."

Sharon grabbed the bill. "This one's on me. Thanks for trusting me enough to open up."

"Now that I've poured my heart out, I could use some salt air to clear my head on the way back home."

"And I gotta grab my stuff and head back to Caldwell. My dad becomes quite the curmudgeon when I'm away too long."

They walked in silence back to the condo, enjoying the warm sun and the gull songs over the waves. By the time Sharon was back on the highway she wondered if Kelly would make the call. *Sounds like she's close. Please let him meet her halfway — she clearly wants him back.*

CHAPTER TWELVE

Elena was having a bad day at adult daycare, and Hannah intercepted her at the door for the third time. "Elena, it's not time to leave yet; you don't want to miss out on apple pie, do you?"

Elena had her coat on and was fiddling with her purse. "I have to pick Carla up. She can't walk home alone."

"But Carla's at work, Elena."

More fiddling. "No, she's at school, and I have to be there before they all leave."

I swear I spend half of my day lying to you, but redirection is the only thing that works. "Tell you what, Elena. I'll call the school and ask if she can stay a little later, so you can help me slice the apples before you go. Could you do that for me?"

"Apples?"

"Remember? We're making a pie, and I don't know anyone that slices apples better than you do."

"Oh....you like them nice and thin?"

"Exactly, Elena! Do you think you could help me? They're Granny Smith." As she spoke, she gently took Elena's arm, who was now engrossed in the conversation.

"The best kind for pie; they don't get mushy."

As they began their way back down the hall, JJ was standing and watching. "Hello, ladies. What's this talk about a pie?"

Elena's expression brightened. "Apple. With Granny Smith. You come by in a bit and have some if you'd like."

JJ flashed her a smile. "I may do that – I hear you're the best baker in town."

"Thank you," Hannah whispered as they passed by. "And do stop by later for a piece."

"Hey, I don't work today—I might take you up on that offer."

He picked up his tool chest and headed down the hall as Hannah turned her attention back to Elena and the others waiting in the kitchen. *He's off today; I wonder if Carla knows. I hope not – tonight's not the night I wanna have Elena to deal with.*

Later that afternoon, Elena had forgotten all about her earlier escape attempts. After reminiscing with the others about late summer activities and how hot the kitchen got while baking, Hannah was thrilled to hand JJ a slice while still warm.

"Sit and eat," Hannah said. "No need to stand up in the corner."

"Can you join me?"

Hannah nodded, grabbing her own piece and a fork. "For a few minutes. They're all occupied."

"You're so good with them – especially Elena. Carla's grandmother, right?"

"Hmm-mm. She's like an adopted grandmother, being right across the street my whole life. I spent a lot of time over there when my mom had to stay late at school for something. I hate watching her slip away."

"Yeah, I caught that conversation earlier. I take it she didn't have to pick Carla up."

Hannah enjoyed a bite of pie before answering. "She used to – everyday. Carla's mom left when she was seven, so she'd drop her off at school and then work at the fish factory all day before picking her up. Rain or shine, she'd be waiting to walk Carla home."

"Does she try to leave every day?"

Hannah shook her head. "Only on bad days, which are unfortunately increasing in number. Might be an interesting walk home."

"You walk her here and back every day?"

"When the weather's nice. Otherwise, I drive her."

"And then she's home alone?"

"Carla lives with her – she's the night shift, unless she has to work late, or needs a break."

JJ got quiet as he ate his pie. "Maybe that explains it."

"Huh?"

"I ran into her this week, and she said we needed to hang out some night. Guess she needs a break?"

Careful, Hannah. Don't say anything that'll come back to bite you later. "Always. She works hard all day and then babysits an old lady when her friends are going out. I'm sure she'd love nothing more than to kick back and relax."

JJ's jaw stiffened a bit. "It's just that..." He caught Hannah's gaze and fumbled with his words. "I don't go to bars anymore – I can't, actually."

Hannah tried to be casual. "I suspect there's lots more to do besides bar-hopping."

JJ sighed. "That's kind of what I'm afraid of. I don't wanna give Carla any ideas or mixed signals. I suspect she'd like a whole lot more from me than I'd be interested in giving...if you know what I mean."

Loud and clear, pal. And your suspicions are spot on. "Easier to avoid her than to hurt her feelings?"

"Yeah. I mean, there's nothing *wrong* with her, but she makes me nervous – most girls do lately. Except for maybe you."

"Not sure if I should be offended by that," Hannah teased. "Hold on a sec." She hopped up and approached an elderly man putting his dish in the sink. "Are you all done, Ronald?"

"I am. It was delicious. I have to find my wallet so I can give you a tip."

"You know what? Pie is on the house today; how 'bout that? And if you could stay a few minutes longer, I would love your help on a cross-word puzzle I've been working on. Think I could pick your brain?"

The old man brushed a few pie crumbs off of his sweatshirt. "Sure! What's the clue?"

Hannah glanced back at JJ. "Afraid our chat is over. Duty calls. Glad you enjoyed the pie." Turning back toward the old man, She smiled. "Why don't we help the others clear their plates and we can go tackle it together. Does that work?"

"Only a few minutes, though. I have to head out soon."

"A few minutes it is. Elena, we're all going to help Ronald with his crossword puzzle. Can you walk with me and tell me how the pie was?"

She waved at JJ as she gathered the half dozen clients and escorted them down the hall.

Hours later, she was surprised to find JJ heading out the door just as she and Elena were leaving. "You stayed late today. Do you earn brownie points from the warden?"

He grinned. "One can hope. I offered to make a couple of new bookshelves for the library, and with no work today I was able to finish them – aside from the staining."

As they reached his bike, Elena ran her frail hand over the seat. "This is a beauty. So shiny."

"Would you like a ride, Elena? I can drive you home."

Elena laughed out loud, studying JJ's face. "You're Arlene's boy, aren't you? Now you stay out of trouble – and wear a helmet."

And just like that, she has moments of total clarity. Like a curtain that opens on a fully functioning brain again. She gently took the old woman's arm. "I think JJ wants to go home, Elena, and we should, too." She continued as JJ put his helmet on and straddled his bike. "Catch you round, I guess."

JJ paused, shifting his weight from one foot to the other. "Hey, what are you doing this Saturday? I have the day off."

Hannah's pulse quickened, the memory of riding on his bike still with her. "You wouldn't believe it if I told you."

"Try me."

"I'm going to a Tiny House Expo in Danvers."

JJ's face lit up. "No way! I *love* tiny houses!"

"Seriously?" Hannah replied. "Most people think I'm nuts."

"I watch tons of videos online. I, ah...don't suppose I could tag along?"

Hanna only paused a second. "Sure – I'd like that. Give me your number tomorrow and we can finalize plans. We'll need to leave by eight sharp."

"Not a problem. And thanks – I've been wanting to tour one for years."

Elena ended their conversation. "Time to go now, Hannah." As they strolled past JJ, she added, "Now you be a gentleman, young man, understand?"

JJ grinned. "You bet, Elena. The lady deserves nothing less."

All the way home, Hannah listened to Elena chat about all the flowers they passed. The older woman had always wanted to garden, but working full time to support her grand-daughter didn't allow much time for it. However, she admired every flower they passed by, and by the time they reached Elena's house, Hannah was glad to have conversation end.

Carla was home already, banging pots and pans and slamming cabinet doors.

I guess Elena's not the only one having a bad day. "Hey, *you're* home early."

Her friend slammed yet another door after grabbing a jar of spaghetti sauce. "Yeah – nothing like having a night off and spending it at home." Her tone softened a bit when her greeted Elena. "Hi, Nonna. Did you have a nice time today?"

"We did! I made an apple pie and it was delicious."

Carla glanced at Hannah for confirmation before continuing. "Sounds delicious. Did you bring me some?"

Elena looked distraught. "I...didn't. I... could go back and see if they have any left."

"Never mind, Nonna. I'll buy apples tomorrow and make one for the weekend. Why don't you watch television while I make some spaghetti?"

"Hmm...spaghetti's my favorite." Without another word, Elena walked into the living room and turned on the television before sitting in her favorite cushioned rocking chair.

Carla filled a big pot with water and put it on the stove. "How was she today?"

"More agitated than usual. Tried to leave twice to pick you up. Doesn't look like you had a great day, either."

Carla took her frustration out on the onion she was chopping. "I can't wait to get outta this damn town and have a life."

"Wanna talk?"

"Nothing to tell – not a *damn* thing." She sniffled a bit, but Hannah wasn't sure if it was emotions or the onions, so she waited. "I finally saw JJ the other day, and asked if he wanted to hang out sometime." She poured a bit of oil into a pan and added the onion, stirring as it sizzled. "A lot of good *that* did."

"I take it he turned you down?"

"Hell, he was nice about it, but it was obvious he had no desire to hook up." She practically threw the spaghetti into the pot. "I swear there isn't a decent guy left in this friggin' town."

"Sorry."

"Whatever. Looks like I won't need you to cover the night shift for me – could you come Saturday instead? I could use a break."

Hannah sighed. "I can't during the day. I have that Tiny House expo, remember?"

Carla took a couple of plates out of the cabinet before slamming more doors. "Of *course* you do. Everyone has a life except me."

"Come on – the expo's been on my calendar for months. I can come Sunday, though."

"Mom's coming Sunday – for her weekly appearance – and to flaunt her man in front of me. Maybe I should ask if *he's* interested – he certainly has an appetite."

"Ew! He's in his forties at least – and he's screwing your mom!"

Carla stirred the pasta. "You think I care about her feelings? Has she ever cared about mine? Might be fun to screw her over like she did to me."

"That grosses me out on way too many levels. I'm gonna head home." She called in to Elena, but the older woman was entranced by

Wheel of Fortune reruns. "Please tell me you won't pursue that idea. There are other guys in town who are way better choices."

Carla didn't say anything as she prepared a plate for Elena and placed it on the table. "Nonna! Come on in; dinner's all ready." As she waited for her grandmother, she turned to Hannah. "All I know is I'm gonna get laid this weekend one way or another. Maybe I'll track JJ down and try being a little more persuasive."

"JJ?" Elena said as she sat down. "He looked nice today."

Carla kissed her head and handed her a fork. "Yup, he sure did, Nonna." Turning back to Hannah, she continued. "She doesn't have any sense of reality anymore. I feel like I'm living in a bad sci-fi movie – one that never ends."

She thinks Elena's out of it again. Rather than set her straight, she said goodbye and slipped out the door quietly. *Not in the mood for that shit storm tonight. It'll have to wait.*

CHAPTER THIRTEEN

Jean McBride was sitting on her front porch with coffee when Hannah came out with her tea and banana bread. "I smelled it from the studio earlier. You slept in a bit this morning."

"Got home late. I drove JJ home after the Expo and ended up staying to eat and talk with him and Vinny. Sorry I didn't text you."

Jean took a bite of the banana bread and enjoyed the sweet flavors. "I wasn't worried; never have been about you. So how was the Expo?"

Hannah's face lit up. "I was in heaven! There were ten different houses – all different styles and builders—and every one was gorgeous! JJ was laughing at me because I was so excited."

"And what did he think?"

"He talked to each of the builders forever, and noted all the architectural choices and finishing touches in each model. I think he'd love building houses – or anything else, for that matter."

"Something to explore when he's done with community service."

Hannah sipped her tea pensively. "Maybe...but he's got two strikes against him."

"What do you mean?"

"Well, his arrest record, for one – although he seems totally committed to recovery, and he'd have no trouble taking drug tests to prove it."

"What's the other?"

"No diploma."

Jean nodded. "I remember; he dropped out his junior year when he left town. And he's right; most places won't hire without one."

"It's a shame; he's super smart."

"Always was. He always knew more than his classmates—and *loved* studying architecture in Art History." She paused to take another bite. "He should get his GED."

Hannah agreed. "I told him the same thing! Even offered to tutor him. I'll have to explore—"

"Where the hell is she going?" Jean put her cup down and bolted down the stairs.

Across the street, Elena headed down the sidewalk in her house-coat and slippers, her purse draped over her shoulder. Hannah joined her mom, noting that Carla's car wasn't in the driveway.

Jean reached her first. "Elena! Where are you heading so early?"

The older woman turned, smiling at Jean. "Good morning! I can't talk, I'm late for work."

"But Elena," Hannah said, "You can't wear your housecoat, can you?"

Elena, all flustered, looked down at her attire. "Oh, dear! I forgot to change again. I...I get so confused sometimes."

Jean took her hand as they walked back. "Honey, we all do as we get older."

Hannah closed the door behind them, noting the television evange-list flailing his arms around. "How about I help you pick out an outfit and mom can make you some coffee?"

"That would be lovely," Elena whispered, fumbling with her house-coat buttons.

"What's that smell?" Jean turned off the television and hurried to the kitchen. *Jesus! She might have set the house on fire!* She grabbed a dish towel inches away from a red-hot coil on the stove before turning the water faucet off. A small pan with burnt globs of oatmeal sat in the sink with assorted measuring cups and silverware. *Where the hell is Carla?*

She had food ready by the time the others returned. "Thought you might like some of Hannah's strawberry jam on your toast."

"Hmm...smells delicious," Elena said as she sat down. "I didn't have time for breakfast this morning." As she ate, Jean pointed out the pot in the sink and showed Hannah where the dish towel had been.

Carla's sputtering engine announced her arrival, and she was surprised to find her neighbors in the kitchen. "Hey, what are you guys doing here? Morning, Nonna; I see they made you breakfast. I have to change for work. " She kissed her grandmother's cheek before catching Hannah's glare. "What's with the angry eyes?"

Jean interrupted. "Why don't we take this discussion into the other room?"

Carla led them into the living room, spinning around to face them. "Look, I don't have much time to—"

"You better *make* some time! "Where the hell have you been?" Hannah hissed, noticing Carla's unkempt hair. "Wait a minute; were you gone all night?"

"She was asleep when I left," Carla replied defensively, "and she usually watches television in the morning. What's the big deal?"

Hannah stepped forward and tapped her chest forcefully. "The big deal," she spat out in a whisper, "is that when you were out screwing around with whoever you hooked up with last night, your grandmother left the house in her nightgown and almost set the house on fire!"

Carla crumbled onto the couch, her eyes filling with tears. "Shit."

Before Hannah continued, Jean put her hand up and sat down on the couch. "Honey, I realize how hard it is being her primary caregiver, and how tired you must be. But today might have been a true emergency if we hadn't been sitting out on the porch."

"What happened?"

"She headed down the street in her nightgown. Said she was going to work. She left the door open, the tv blaring, the water running, and the stove on with a dish towel inches away from the burner. The house could have gone up in flames."

Carla hid her face in her hands. "I can't take this anymore. She's getting worse every day. I never would have left her if I'd known—"

"That's just it; you never *will* know. She's not safe being alone anymore – you need to explore assisted living."

"But she's lived in this house her whole life."

Hannah sat down on the chair beside her friend, her mood more sympathetic. "But she won't remember that much longer."

"My mom should have moved back in here to help. Then maybe Nonna could stay."

Jean's jaw tightened. "I intend to have a long talk with your mother about not doing her part – and letting you carry the weight yourself. She should know better by now."

Carla wiped her tears away. "Yeah, well I'm used to it," she said bitterly. "Look, I wanna go check on Nonna, okay? I'll call work and tell 'em I'll be late. I won't leave her till my mom shows up."

Jean shook her head. "You head into work. I'll stay with her. No time like the present to have that little chat."

An hour later, Jean sat with Elena as they ate the lunch she'd prepared. About halfway through their meal, Jean spotted Betty Sue coming in the front door carrying a pizza box.

"Mother, it's Betty Sue! I brought us pizza for lun—" She spotted Jean as she walked toward the kitchen. "Why, *hello* neighbor! I didn't know you were going to be here today. And what a delicious meal you've cooked!" She leaned down to give Elena a kiss on the cheek. "Hello, mother. I guess we don't need this old pizza with chicken alfredo on the table."

Elena put her fork down. "Sit down and I'll fix you a plate."

Betty Sue patted her shoulder. "Don't you worry your pretty little head about that; I'll help myself– and we'll save the pizza for when Sean gets here."

Jean's ears perked up. "Ah, the beau is coming back, is he?"

Betty Sue sat down with some alfredo as she replied. "He was busy all day yesterday, and since I *had* to be here today, I convinced him to come and visit. If I'd known you were here, I would have met him for brunch somewhere."

"Ah, stop your pouting. My visit wasn't planned, and we have some things to talk about before your boyfriend gets here." She glanced over at Elena. "Let's wait until after she's done and settled, shall we? In the meantime, tell us all about that romance of yours."

"He is just the *perfect* man for me. I can't believe how fortunate I am to be blessed with another treasure. When poor Kenneth died, God rest his soul, I thought I'd be a lonely old widow like my mother —and you, for that matter."

Jean almost choked on her water. "Excuse me? I may be old, and Adam may be deceased, but I'm sure as hell not lonely without him. He was anything *but* a treasure! Hell, you were married to Brad before Ken came along, so you should know all about cheating husbands."

"Well, that ended with Kenneth. He was the most devoted husband I could have asked for, and gave me everything I wanted."

"Everything? How 'bout your little girl? He had no trouble saying no to Carla —or maybe she wasn't something *you* wanted at the time."

Betty Sue glared at her. "She was all settled here--and happy. Ken had lots of business travels planned and it would have been impossible to keep up with her schooling if we were dragging her around Europe. Besides, she kept Mother company." She reached over to pat Elena's hand. "Carla loves her Nonna, doesn't she?"

The older woman smiled. "She's a good girl. Are you taking her back to Tennessee finally?"

Jean smirked. *You go, Elena. Even with dementia you manage a barb.*

"Mother, I don't *live* in Tennessee anymore," Betty answered with frustration. "I live in my townhouse by the harbor, remember?"

Elena ran her finger along the bottom of her plate and licked the remaining alfredo sauce. "That was yummy. I think I'm gonna lie down now."

"You've earned a nap, Elena, after your busy morning. I'll help Betty Sue clean up."

Jean waited until she had walked down the hall, then faced her neighbor with a solemn expression. "We've gotta talk." She filled Betty

Sue in on what had happened earlier. "She's going downhill fast. You and Carla need to make some decisions, and soon. She can't be alone anymore – not even for a few minutes."

"So, you mean to tell me that my daughter left her alone all night? Wait till I get—"

"Oh, for God's sake, lay off of Carla! She's here every single night from dinner time on, and is out the door to waitress or clean almost every morning. If *anyone* should be stepping up right now, it's *you!* You're the one with all the time on your hands, and yet you think popping in a few times a week is enough."

Betty's eyes flashed anger. "I am *hardly* sitting at home twirling my thumbs all day; I have a busy life and come here as often as I can – and I'm on the phone with her a million times a day."

Jean leaned forward. "She almost set the house on fire this morning. Is that what you're hoping for, so you won't have to deal with her *or* Carla?"

"How *dare* you! You have no idea how—"

The doorbell cut her off, and Betty Sue's mood changed in an instant. "That'll be Sean! We'll have to talk about this later!" She scooted through the living room and into the arms of Sean McClean, throwing her arms around him and planting a wet kiss as he grabbed her butt and squeezed.

And then there's him, who has you wrapped around his little finger. How the hell are we gonna pull you away from him before something bad happens to you as well?

"Hell-o, my sugar," Sean said huskily. "Have you missed me?" He looked around the room, not spotting Jean in the kitchen. "So, where's the old lady?"

"She's taking a little nap."

"Oh, *is* she now?" Sean's hands reached for her butt again, but this time inside her pants. "Let's make use of—"

Oh, the hell you will! Jean turned away from the door and coughed really loudly as she turned the faucet on full blast. Romantic chatter ceased quickly in the other room.

"Now, sweetie, you just hold that thought," Betty Sue said as she hugged Sean's arm and brought him toward the kitchen. "My neighbor Jean was here visiting when I arrived. I'm sure she'll be heading home any time, but you can say hi."

Jean reached for a dish towel as she hid her smirk. "Well, hello there. I hope I didn't thwart your plans too much, but we had a situation here this morning that needed attention. Nice to see you again, Sean."

"Delighted," Sean said, extending his hand. "Sorry if you heard my bad manners in there...but this gorgeous woman here is all I can think about when I'm away from her."

"Oh, *you*," Betty Sue murmured. "Didn't I tell you he was the perfect man for me? Such a romantic!"

Sean spotted the pizza. "Did you bring that for me, sugar?" He opened the box, pulling a slice out and taking a bite. "She bought my favorite – I love it almost as much as I love her! You want a bite?"

Oh, Lord, he's pathetic. And yet she's practically drooling over him as he feeds her. Determined to keep the romance from getting too heated while Elena slept, Jean redirected the conversation back to her reason for being there.

"So, Betty Sue and I were discussing Elena's dementia before you arrived. She's at the point where she needs someone here around the clock, and I suggested Betty and Carla explore full time coverage, or another place to live."

Betty shook her head. "No need to bore my man with all those details right now."

Sean reached for a second piece of pizza. "No, no, no...I'm not at all bored. And I think Jean is spot on. Your mom needs us. We might consider looking for a bigger place. One we could *all* live in--then she'd always have someone around."

"Sean!" Betty said with excitement. "Did you just propose to me?"

Jean almost laughed at the moment of Sean's panic, but he responded with his saccharin reply. "Well, sugar – I'm not sure we're quite ready for *that* step yet, but we've certainly reached the point of wanting to be together night and day...after moving in we'd have time to plan something special."

"Didn't I *tell* you he was perfect?" Betty planted a huge kiss on Sean's cheek and beamed at Jean. "I guess I should call Kelly and have her start checking various places. She's the best realtor on Cape Ann, after all."

Sean answered without bothering to swallow his mouthful of pizza. "Tell you what, Sugar. How about you give me her number." He coughed as a bit as the crust caught in his throat on the way down. "I'd love to surprise you with a dream house just for us."

"Ahem....don't you mean for the *four* of you?" *I'm liking this guy less and less the longer I'm around him.*

"Well of *course* he did. He just said Mother wouldn't have to be alone anymore. Sorry for my neighbor's bad manners. Ooh...you have a little sauce there on your chin, sweetie...let me get it for you."

Betty reached for a napkin, but Sean caught her hand and leaned in. "Save paper and be creative."

"Oh, *you*..." she giggled before licking his face clean and getting a kiss in return.

"Let's save that for later, sugar...I think we should pursue Jean's idea about your mom needing more help. After all, we'd hate for anything to happen to her." He wrapped his arm around her and spoke with a serious and concerned tone. "For instance, with her mind going so fast, you should consider obtaining power of attorney as well – so you can make those all-important decisions if she can't."

Jean bristled. *Damn! Now he's crossing a line that might be more dangerous to Elena than her living here alone. And I don't trust him for a second.* "I think Betty and *Carla* need to make those plans. After all, Carla's been Elena's primary caregiver for years."

"Well, he *knows* that," Betty corrected. "We'll sit down with Carla real soon. I'll call Arlene; her husband Jim's a lawyer, and I'm sure he can handle everything for us. Once Carla agrees, of course." She closed the pizza box and wiped Sean's lips with her finger, catching one more stray bit of sauce, before turning toward Jean. "We'll talk later; you can head on home now, and I'll take care of the rest of the dishes. Thank you for being here earlier – you're a good friend and neighbor, Jean."

Knowing she was being dismissed, Jean reluctantly said goodbye.

"I'm sure Elena will be up any minute; she never sleeps for very long anymore." Hoping it would at least curtail any afternoon romps, she slipped out the back door and walked across the street in a huff. *I gotta call Kelly, so we can start 'Operation Sean be Gone' right away. Betty's thrown all caution and sense out the window — it's up to the brunch club to save her.*

CHAPTER FOURTEEN

Jean showed up at Kelly's the next morning with coffee and donuts, letting herself in the unlocked screen door. Chianti greeted her – first with a protective bark, and then a wagging tail and welcoming circles around her feet. "Morning, handsome."

"We're up here," Kelly called, and Jean joined her and Peg at the dining room table.

"Morning, Peg – thought you were working today."

"Later this morning – have to cover some damn charity event at the hospital at noon. So sick of these community events; the new editor is a sexist ass who doesn't believe women can cover the real news.

"He'd probably hit it off with our Mr. McClean. Hopefully this is a job you can sink your teeth into."

"Hey, Kelly called me last night after talking to you, and I'm in. Let's take this piece of crap down."

Kelly opened her notebook to the ideas the gang had come up with during their first session with Sharon present. "For now, the three of us will proceed– and Sharon when she can come up. Terri's scheduled for lots of physical therapy for her sciatica, and Arlene's afraid she'll blurt something out to Betty Sue."

"Makes sense," Jean said. "She'll still tell us if Betty Sue calls her about the power of attorney. I'm worried about Sean convincing Betty Sue to have Elena sign that over. They could sell the house, stick Elena in a nursing home, and leave Carla with nothing."

"Shit, Betty Sue wouldn't stoop that low," Peg griped. "On *some* level she still loves them."

"True," Jean rebuked, "but right now she's thinking with her hormones, not her head. I don't trust Sean one bit — just a gut feeling."

"Do we even know where he lives or what he does for a living?"

"Not really," Jean said. "Betty Sue says he has a few projects he's working on, and is lining up investors for some big jobs, but she's never asked for details."

Kelly jotted down some notes. "Peg? You can do some research on our buddy. He worked with Sharon's husband Steve for years, but see what else is out there with his name on it."

"Got it."

"Jean, find out what you can regarding Elena's current legal affairs. Maybe talk to Carla. If not, we might need to talk to Arlene's husband."

"I don't remember Carla ever mentioning anything being done, but after yesterday's fiasco, I think she's ready to pursue that — I trust her a lot more than her mother to take care of Elena."

"Agreed. As for me, I'm expecting a call from Sean about real estate, so I'll try to grill him a bit about his current living situation. In the meantime, I'll check on any past real estate deeds." Kelly closed her notebook. "Here's to saving Betty Sue's fortune — and being there to pick up the pieces after we break her heart."

"Ouch," Jean replied. "I wish we could pull it off without that last part. She really has been happy for the first time since Ken died."

"He's gonna break her heart no matter what — for all we know, she's one of the investors he's working on right now."

Jean's coffee stopped mid-air. "Peg, you may be on to something. What if he's working on other women at the same time — especially rich widows?"

Peg's face lit up. "*Now* we're talking about a juicy story. Soon as I'm done at the hospital, I'm on it. Kelly, I'll need a list of all recent real estate transactions in the area – I'll check to see if any match up with recent obituaries. Wouldn't it be awesome if Mr. McClean was a major con man? Damn, I hope so."

As Jean drove home her head was swirling with questions. *What if we're wrong about him, and he's legit? And what will he do if he finds out we're checking him out?* She decided to stop at the Even Keel, the pub where Carla waitressed. *It shouldn't be too busy – mostly locals this time of day. I can sit at the bar and chat.*

She hadn't been in the pub for months, but the place hadn't changed in years. Carla was serving food to a booth halfway down, and only a couple others were occupied. Three older men sat at the other end of the bar – probably retired fishermen who had no place else to be.

Carla threw her tray on top of the bar shelf when she returned, her face displaying concern the moment she saw Jean. "Is Nonna okay?" she asked as her pace increased.

Jean put her hand up. "She's fine. Didn't mean to alarm you."

"You're not exactly a regular customer in here. Everything okay?"

Jean nodded. "Does Joey still make his fish and chips basket? I could go for that today."

"You came in for Joey's fish and chips? That's a bunch of bull."

"Okay, guilty as charged. I came in to chat – but I always ordered that in the old days."

"Trust me, it'll be just as good. Joey's the bomb in the kitchen. You want something to drink with that?"

"I better stick with water. And don't let me keep you from any work, okay?"

Carla laughed. "Those guys? They could walk around the bar and refill their glasses and I wouldn't bat an eye. Been perched on those same stools since long before I was born. The other few tables are set for now. Let me put your order in and I'll be right back."

She disappeared into the kitchen for a minute, returning to check on the three guys at the end, and then pulled up a stool on the other side after getting two glasses of water. "Kinda nice to put my feet up for a few. Food won't take long. So, what's up?"

Jean wasn't exactly sure how to begin. "First off, what do you think of your mom's new guy?"

"Jeez, did she put you up to this?"

"She has no idea I'm here – I want your take on the guy."

"Hell, what I think of him doesn't mean crap – if she wants to throw her life—"

"Carla, this isn't about what she thinks of him. I'm asking what *you* think of him. Some of us aren't convinced that he's the best guy for your mom."

"Honestly? I don't know what the hell she sees in him. He's not much to look at, and she pays when they go out. Maybe he's good in bed – or her standards aren't much higher than mine."

"Carla – don't put yourself down."

"Mrs. McBride, you've known me all my life. I'm the girl guys hook up with, but never date. Once you have a certain reputation in this town, it sorta sticks. Hey, let me check on my last booth and grab your food."

Jean watched her make the rounds, checking with each table and the three regulars. She brought back change to one booth, and then zipped into the kitchen and came back out with a basket laden with fried haddock and fries, along with a small dish of coleslaw and another with tartar sauce.

"Smells as good as ever – it might come back to bite me later, but I'm gonna enjoy this."

Carla chuckled as she hopped back up on the stool. "Joey's the only reason this place survived; doesn't attract the tourists, but the locals keep coming back for his food, and it's been enough for him to live on."

"Wanna help me with the fries? Not sure I'll eat 'em all."

Carla reached for one, blowing on it before popping it in her mouth. "So, the whole gang met Sean, huh? I'm surprised he didn't get higher marks – he can turn on the charm when he wants to."

"But it seems fake. There's something about him we don't like, and we're gonna dig a little to see what we can find."

Carla grinned. "You came in to ask me to spy on my mother? When do I start?"

"Actually, I'm here to ask you a couple things about your grandmother."

"Nonna? What do you wanna know?"

"With her memory declining, is she still in charge of the house accounts?"

Carla shook her head. "Nawh, she added my name to the checking account a long time ago. Her social security is a direct deposit, and I add in whatever's needed for bills. The rest goes into my own account. You guys aren't doubting me, are you?"

Jean shook her head. "God, no. You've been more a daughter to her than your mom has been."

"It kills me to see her slip away. She's the only reason I stay in this town."

"Which leads to my next question. Has Elena made out a will? Because the longer she waits, the more likely—"

"I'm pretty sure she did. Back around the time I started helping with the money, Mr. Winston was at the house one night and she was signing all kinds of papers. I'm not positive it was a will; hell, I'm not sure she'd remember if I asked her."

"Does she have a safety deposit box? Or a place in the house where she'd keep important papers?"

Carla scanned the room, and jumped off the stool. "Hold that thought. Gotta take care of that last booth."

For all her faults, that girl loves her Nonna. God forbid if Elena didn't make out a will, or has to sell the house for assisted living – or worse yet, if everything goes to Betty Sue and Carla gets nothing.

Carla returned within a few minutes, but rather than sit again, she pushed the stool back under the bar. "Much as I'd love to visit more, I have to wrap some silverware. But I did think of something. Nonna has an old tin box from my grandpa; she keeps it under her bed. I can pull it out sometime and take a look – I imagine that's where she'd keep anything important."

Jean slipped a twenty onto the counter. "You're a good kid, Carla Douglas – don't you forget it. And keep the change."

Carla swallowed hard. "Okay. And Mrs. McBride? Thanks for always being an adopted mom; Hannah's so lucky to have you." As Jean got up to leave, Carla grinned. "And I'll keep my eyes and ears open when it comes to Sean – and Nonna, too."

Jean smiled. "Thanks, Carla. Was nice to catch up." She left the *Even Keel* hopeful. Carla's motives weren't as positive as her own, but if there was dirt to be found on Sean McClean, Carla might be just the one to find it – if only to screw her mother back.

CHAPTER FIFTEEN

The following Friday, Betty Sue was snuggled up next to Sean on the couch watching *Dirty Rotten Scoundrels* after a sumptuous meal of lobster casserole with fresh bread and salad. They sipped their wine and shared kisses as his hand occasionally reached down to cup her breast. "Soon as our bellies digest dinner," he whispered, "I'm gonna enjoy my dessert even more, sugar."

"You are insatiable," she teased, patting his belly. "I believe you had dessert *before* dinner."

"*That* was my appetizer," he said, his voice getting husky. "And you were a vixen." His thumb caressed the outside of her silk robe until she shivered.

She sat up a bit and reached for her wine, her face flushed. "God, I'm horny all the time these days."

"Maybe you're just having another hot flash."

Betty Sue fanned her cheeks. "Oh, I am – but I don't think this one has anything to do with menopause. I'm glad you got here early today. Gave us some extra time together."

"Especially with you running off tomorrow and leaving me all alone." Sean faked a pout.

"Oh, you *know* I hate leaving you. But Arlene's been so excited about her fancy women's brunch, and she can't stand going alone with nobody to sit with."

"She's not vivacious like you, that's for sure."

"Hardly! Don't get me wrong; Jim's a wonderful provider, and they have a lovely home. But he expects her to be a submissive wife who maintains the household and has dinner ready every night. It helps that she has very simple tastes, but she really doesn't get out much."

"So, what's this fancy brunch she's dragging you to?"

"Up at the Elks – they have a quarterly brunch for the women members and their guests, and then discuss programming ideas for the upcoming months. It's one of the places she's free to help out with – there, and church."

"You'd think she'd make some friends in both of those places."

Betty Sue shook her head. "Arlene's got a heart of gold, and will pray for anyone who needs it, but she's so quiet and a bit insecure, so it's hard for her to meet new people. Kelly and I have been her closest friends for years, and she doesn't seem to need more than our little gang."

She snuggled in close. "And I'm *sure* she doesn't get the loving from Jim like I have right here." She patted his belly again lovingly, and he moved her hand lower as he pulled her closer.

"I think what you have right here is ready for round two," he said, nibbling her neck. "Let's go back to bed, sugar..."

Giggling like a school girl, she climbed on his lap and kissed his nose, pulling her robe off as she moved. "I think we can manage right here, right now," she whispered.

Sean grunted. "*Now* who's insatiable, sugar?"

* * *

She was still smiling the next morning, applying mascara while he watched from tussled sheets. "I must say, you look mighty fine in my bed. Makes it hard to drag myself away."

He laughed and patted the spot beside him. "You could always stay."

"Don't you tempt me," she teased, brushing her curls out. "But I'll make it up to ya when I get home. Drink some coffee and grab something to eat while I'm gone – to keep your strength up."

Sean laughed. "Coffee's always good, and I can sit outside and watch—"

"Oh, dang!" Betty Sue grabbed her shoes. "I was gonna stop next door and open up the screen door to the deck. I don't know if you remember my friend Sharon from the party – her son owns the townhouse – and she's due to arrive later this morning. I usually air the place out a bit for her."

A smile crept on to Sean's face. "Sugar, if it would help, I'd be happy to take care of that. Least I could do since I'm the one making you late."

She stood up and tucked her blouse into her skirt. "Are you sure?" She leaned over and gave him a kiss on the forehead. "You are the most thoughtful man I've ever known. And don't fuss over there; Carla cleaned it, so it just needs some fresh air. I'll leave the key for you on the counter – it's labeled 'Tim's townhouse'-- and I'll be back as fast as I can manage."

As the door closed, Sean laughed out loud. *Ate lobster, got laid three times, and now I have the key for next door. What a mighty fine day.* After getting dressed, he poured a cup of coffee and picked up the key. *But before I go, might as well explore.* He sat down at Betty Sue's desk, rifling through the drawers until he found the bank file. Opening the folder, he whistled softly at the most current statement. He scanned through the papers in the folder and laughed out loud as he grabbed a pen and note pad. *And you're stupid enough to leave your password right here, sugar.* Scribbling down the information, he tucked it in his pocket and put the folder away. "I'll tend to this later – right now, it's time to greet an old friend." *Oh, it's one mighty fine day, indeed.*

      * * *

Betty Sue was enjoying her brunch, and it warmed her heart to see Arlene smiling and laughing. "You're such a dear friend, Arlene; and all those prayers you said for me after losing Ken are finally being answered. You must have prayed Sean right into my life."

Arlene sat quietly, fiddling with her wedding band. "I doubt I had anything to do with that."

"Don't doubt yourself. Sometimes I wish I had your faith; you're one of most loyal and trustworthy women in town – and I'm so grateful for the invite today."

Arlene smiled uncomfortably. "I'm...glad you could come."

"I wish Kelly had joined us – I'm dying to find out if Sean called her yet."

Flustered, Arlene lost her grip on her fork as it clattered onto her plate. "Sean's calling Kelly?"

Betty sipped her mimosa, unbothered by the noise. "He sure is. He's looking for a bigger place for us." She leaned forward, her voice more animated. "I think he might be popping the question before long!"

Arlene sat back startled. "Oh my! I mean..." The fiddling with her wedding band intensified.

"My goodness, Arlene. What is going on in that pretty little head of yours? You seem so flustered. Did they bring you a mimosa by mistake?"

"No....I'm fine. Really. But aren't you rushing things a bit with Sean? You don't really know him that well yet."

Betty Sue laughed, flagging the waitress down for another drink. "Oh, honey, after last night and this morning, I can assure you I know every little inch of my new sweetie."

She watched her friend blush, and reached out to take her hand. "I'm sorry. I forgot you don't like to talk about life's more intimate moments. So, tell me about Jim. What's he up to these days? Any big cases?"

"He doesn't talk about his work at home; never does. Evenings are for watching television and relaxing."

"And you knit."

Arlene's face relaxed and her smile was genuine. "Nothing gives me more peace. I let him sit there and watch his shows while I focus on the clicking of my needles and the softness of the yarn. My current afghan is the softest yarn I've ever worked with. I can't wait to curl up underneath it when the snow starts flying."

Betty Sue chuckled. "If it brings you that much joy, then keep knitting, my friend." She reached for the newly delivered mimosa. "I only hope that yarn keeps you half as warm as the hot human blanket I'll be wrapped up in."

CHAPTER SIXTEEN

Sharon Collins had made good time on the ride up. *They said after Labor Day things would start getting easier. I guess they were right.* She pulled in to her spot by the townhouse, noticing Betty Sue's car missing. *I'm glad she's out. I could have stayed with Kelly again, but Tim needs me to check on things after having rented the place out last week.* She grabbed her overnight bag and purse, got out and locked the car, and enjoyed the salt air as she walked to the door.

As she entered, she immediately noticed the open screen door. *I do love when she lets the fresh air in for me.* She dropped her bag inside the door and placed her purse on the table, heading straight for the deck and a quick view of the harbor. "I'll never tire of—"

"Hello, Sharon."

She spun to her left, where Sean McClean sat on the double glider, casually sipping a mug of coffee. "What the hell are you doing here?!"

He smirked, taking his time for a long sip as he looked out over the harbor. "Enjoying the view, no doubt."

Sharon stood frozen in place, her heart racing. "How the hell did you get in here?"

Again, that smirk. Sean held up a key with 'Tim's townhouse' on the tag. "My dear Betty was running a little late this morning, so I gallantly offered to come over for her and allow you some fresh air when you arrived. Glad you made it; my coffee's actually cold at this point."

"You've been...waiting for me."

He grinned. "I have." He patted the glider beside him. "There's room for two; wanna join me?"

"When hell freezes over. I'd like you to leave."

Sean stretched his legs out and leaned back, resting his coffee mug on his protruding stomach. "Relax. I won't be here long, but I thought it was time to chat after our reunion at Betty's. You made a wise choice to keep quiet."

"Who says I have?"

Sean laughed. "Come on, Sharon. Betty Sue may be a lot of things, but smart and secretive are not on the list. If you'd told her anything she would have let it slip the first time we were together."

"Maybe I've been waiting for the right time."

"You're bluffing, beautiful. You know damn well there is no right time to divulge our little secret past. After all, you and your dad live in the same house, and you wouldn't want me to show up on your doorstep, now would you?" He chuckled, and then added, "So how is the old man's ticker holding up?"

"You wouldn't dare."

Sean stood up, taking a step toward her as Sharon backed up against the railing. "Is that a challenge, my dear? 'Cause I could drive right down to Caldwell now while you're up here."

Sharon, despite feeling trapped, tried to convey a calm demeanor. "Maybe I've already told him all about your little romance next door – that would certainly take away your edge, wouldn't it?"

Sean laughed, leaning in toward her with a smile. "Oh, my sweet Sharon – how stupid do you think I am? The panic in your eyes makes it real clear that you've kept your mouth shut, so we'll keep it that way – won't we?"

"Are you threatening me now?"

"Wouldn't think of it. But don't ever forget about the *other* things I could tell your old man, my little rosebud. Senior prom—and the summer that followed?"

Sharon leaned against the railing, her legs weak with the mention of his pet name for her.

"I'm sure you've never filled him in on all those nights in the hardware store after hours, have you?" Sean's eyes traveled down Sharon's body. "Oh, you were something, you were. Pretty well preserved, I might add."

"You're a sick man," she spat out.

"Yeah, I wonder how the old man's heart would hold up if he knew I'm the one you lost your virginity to…those were some good times. Almost wish I hadn't introduced you to my college roommate. Who knows? Maybe I would have ended up as Tim's daddy."

"You need to shut up."

"I bet it's been a long time since my little rosebud's felt a man up against her…" Sean cocked his head to one side with a grin. "What do you say? Betty won't be back for a good hour or more."

As he reached out to touch Sharon's cheek, she side stepped away and ran inside, holding on to the counter to support her shaking legs. "Get out. *Now.* Or I'm calling the police." She held up her phone, praying that he wouldn't see her hand trembling.

Sean strolled back in, unfazed. "Relax, okay? I'm just messing with ya. Besides, much as I'd love to get reacquainted, I better pace myself. No doubt Betty Sue will be ready for another round when she gets back – I tell ya, she has *some* appetite after so many years without a man."

"Now you're being disgusting – get *out.*"

"I'm going, sweetheart – but keep your ears open later. I'll be sure we make a lot of noise so you can hear what you're missing. And then I'll convince my little sugar to invite you over for dinner later."

"The hell you will. I won't step foot inside that place until you're long gone. Now *leave* – before I change my mind about calling the police"

Sean twirled the key around on the keychain. "Alright, I'm going…

but be sure to lock that deadbolt nice and tight. You wouldn't want anyone sneaking in tonight while you're asleep."

He laughed as he walked out and closed the door. On shaky legs, Sharon chased after him and fumbled with the deadbolt to lock it in place. She collapsed on the chair closest to the door and tried not to hyperventilate.

Oh, my God. What am I gonna do? I can't stay here with him right next door. I can't. She inhaled sharply as the tears came. Memories of that night, so very long ago, came rushing back. After senior prom he had brought her to the store– where he seduced her for the first time.

She couldn't remember how many times she'd lied to her parents that summer about having to work late so he could be satisfied again and again. He promised he'd teach her how wonderful sex was, but never once tended to her desires, focusing only on the short amount of time needed for his own pleasure.

Her phone ringing made her jump. She saw Tim's name flash on the screen. *Damn. I was supposed to call when I arrived.* She tried to calm her voice as she hit the button to answer.

"Hey there. Sorry I forgot to call."

Tim's voice was warm and charming on the other end. "I was starting to worry a bit; wanted to be sure you didn't run into any trouble."

Oh, God, you have no idea. "Nope; just wanted a little fresh air, that's all."

"You sure, mom? Your voice sounds a little shaky."

"I'm fine. And everything here was in good shape. Carla does a great job cleaning."

"And did Betty Sue have the screen door open when you arrived? She's convinced we all need fresh, salt air to breathe the minute we arrive."

Sharon swallowed hard, determined to keep her voice steady. "She did. Although it wasn't necessary. And shouldn't Carla have the key instead – after all, she's the one who comes in to clean."

"Good idea, mom. Why not ask Betty what she thinks? I'm sure you two will have a blast this weekend. I'll be bringing Maggie back up in a few weeks – maybe even bring Granddad."

"No!" Sharon blurted out. "I mean...not with your new bride?"

Tim chuckled. "True--especially with a late anniversary celebration. I'll let you go. See you tomorrow, Mom. Love you."

"Love you, too, son."

"Drive safe."

"I will. Give Dad and Maggie my love."

She sat there for well over an hour, wondering how in the world she'd be able to keep them from finding out about the big surprise next door. She had to find a way. She had to.

CHAPTER SEVENTEEN

Kelly was finishing up with a showing when her phone rang. "Hey, Sharon! Are you up for the weekend?" As Sharon explained what had transpired with Sean her demeanor changed. "Are you okay? Do you want to come to my place? You shouldn't be alone."

"We need to find a way to get rid of him—the sooner the better. My son's coming up with his wife in the next couple of weeks, and I don't want them to run into each other."

"Give me the dates and I'll figure out how to keep Betty Sue so busy she won't have time to consider entertaining. Trust me, it's not hard."

"I worry about her. She's gonna be hurt."

"The brunch club will help pick up the pieces. Where's the scumbag now? Is he still next door?"

"Oh, yeah. Waiting for his *sugar* to come home—to tend to his needs, no doubt."

"Ew...wait! Is Betty Sue with Arlene at an Elks brunch? I could run over and find out what she's planning for her weekend with him."

"Will she wonder why you're there?"

"Trust me, I can handle Betty Sue. In the meantime, I need to call

Peg. She might be free to drive over to the townhouse and follow Sean when he leaves."

"I pray he's leaving today and not tomorrow. I'll never be able to relax with him over there."

"Like I said, my place is an option if you absolutely need it. I'll let you go for now, and will call later when I have something to report. See you soon, Sharon."

She checked her purse to make sure she still had the coupon for the knitting store. "*A handy excuse for zipping over to the Elks — should be able to catch them before they leave.* As she drove, she called Peg and was surprised to hear how excited she was.

"A stake out!" Haven't done one of those for years! Let me feed the cats and I'll head right over to the townhouse. When he heads out, I'll be right behind him."

"Might be awhile. Let me call you back after I talk to Betty Sue."

"You do that. And I'll pack some sandwiches just in case."

Peg was revved up about work for the first time in ages. *Okay, so it's not actual work, but it reminds me of better days at the Sentinel. If my editor heard I was staking out a possible con man, I'd get more respect.* Parked at the end of the parking lot across from Betty's apartment, she couldn't wait for Sean to leave. An open notebook and pen lay on the seat beside her phone, along with small binoculars and a voice recorder -- both bought at a thrift store decades ago. She was ready.

When Betty Sue walked Sean out to his car for a lengthy goodbye, Peg clicked on the recorder. "3:35: subject is leaving in a black Ford Fusion. Turning left onto Atlantic Rd." She followed him fifteen miles down the coast to the town of Beverly, pulling in to a seedy looking place. "3:55: Subject arrived at Sea View Motel and entered room #4 on ground floor."

She parked close enough to keep an eye on the door and ate a sandwich. *You already had your key, so you're staying here, which tells me you've got something to hide.*

Within a half hour, Peg wiped the crumbs from her shirt and grabbed her recorder as he emerged. "4:32: Subject changed his clothes and appears to have showered. Heading south again towards Salem.

Shit! Get out of my way, you moron – I'm tailing someone!" *Jesus! This guy drives like an old man; I can't afford to lose him.* She breathed a sigh of relief as she spotted him turning onto a quiet, shaded street and into the driveway of a modest home. "4:45. Subject arrived at #129 Lyons Drive and a hot blonde has greeted him at the door." She grabbed her phone and snapped a photo of Sean planting a lengthy kiss with roaming hands.

Well, well, well, Mr. McClean, what have we here? Judging from her greeting I highly doubt that woman is your sister, you scumbag. You were liter- ally in my friend's bed a few hours ago. She got a clear shot of their faces as Sean helped her into his car, and within minutes they arrived at the Harbor Side Yacht Club. *Hell, I remember this place. This is where Kelly and Travis docked their boat; I wonder if he's still here.*

She grabbed a floppy hat and stashed needed items into a bag before finding a bench by the water which provided good visibility. Within minutes they were seated at a table along the railing closest to her. *Bingo! I can see both of your faces...smile for the camera!* She opened a book to hide the voice recorder she was holding in her other hand. "5:30:Subject arrived at Harbor View Yacht Club with female. The latter must be a member as she ordered without opening the menu and chatted with the waiter like she knew him."

An hour later, Sean and his mystery date finished their meal and ordered more wine. Peg recalled the bologna sandwiches in the car as her stomach growled. *Hell, this is way more important than food – most fun I've had in months.* "6:25. Female signed for dinner, and they brought their bottle down the steps toward the marina." *Oh, crap! What if they walk right past me?* Peg yanked the brim of her hat down and buried her face in the book as the couple turned toward a sailboat two slips over. "That was close! They've boarded a large sailboat named *Breakfast at Tiffany's*," she continued, " And they've disappeared below deck without casting off." *Don't take no brains to figure out what's going on down there. Mr. McClean, you are a very naughty boy. And we're gonna love taking you—*

"Peg?" A familiar voice startled her, and the voice recorder slipped out of her hand and down into her bra. *Shit! I can't fish it out right now!*

"Travis! What a surprise!" *God, he's as handsome as ever. Those dark curls...*

"What in the world brings you here?"

"Ah...I had an appointment with someone to talk about a charity thing, but they called and couldn't make it. Thought I'd enjoy a little fresh air before heading home." *What a stupid answer...but hell, he seems to be buying it.* "By the way, do you happen to know who owns that boat over there? The *Breakfast at Tiffany's?* I saw a woman who looked familiar to me, but I can't place her − drives me crazy when I can't remember where I've met someone—but hell, it's a nice boat."

"I'm sure she came across your desk at some point. Name's Tiffany Henderson. The boat was her dad's − he named it after her."

"Was?"

"He passed away about six months ago − cancer. She was his pride and joy − and a bit of a spoiled brat because of it."

"It must have been hard to lose him if they were that close."

Travis chuckled. "Yeah, I'm not sure they were − she was probably way more in love with his bank account. Got every penny, from what I hear."

Before Peg could reply, Sean and Tiffany reappeared on deck giggling as Tiffany began taking selfies with the sun setting behind them.

Shit! He might recognize me! Peg spun around between Travis and the sailboat, keeping her voice low when she spoke. "She doesn't seem to be grieving a whole lot, does she?" *Sean has himself a second woman with tons of money. Ain't that interesting?*

Travis ignored her question and asked one of his own. "Is...Kelly doing okay?"

God, those puppy-dog eyes. Why can't she see how much he wants her back? "She's not dating anyone, if that's what you're asking." She hunched her shoulders forward a bit to allow more space in her cleavage for the recorder. *I don't want this conversation to be muffled by my damn boobs.*

Travis sighed. "Is it that obvious? I tell ya, it still kills me to be here instead of home. I screwed up so bad."

Peg noticed tears, even though he wiped them away quickly. "She still loves you, Travis. You should fight a little harder to win her back."

Travis took a step back as if defeated. "I don't wanna push too hard if she's not ready."

She reached out and touched his arm gently. "But what if she *is* ready, and just scared like you are? Don't wait too long – you guys were too good together to throw it away."

"Thanks, Peg. I'm glad I ran into you. Gives me a lot to think about."

"Good seeing you, too. Take care of yourself, okay?" Peg took a glance over her shoulder, relieved that Sean and his date were below deck again. *Might have been a fiasco if he recognized me. God, I can't wait to get this recorder out of my bra!*

Travis nodded as he turned and walked to the next slip to where the *Dreamweaver* was tied. He waved as he stepped on board. Peg returned the wave and returned to her car. She sat munching her last bologna sandwich as she retrieved the recorder, checking to see if the final conversation was clear. *Kelly might need to hear it herself – then she'll realize how much he still loves her.*

CHAPTER EIGHTEEN

Kelly picked up on the first ring. "Hi, Peg; we were just talking about you. Guess you don't check your messages regularly."

"Had my phone turned off. Who are you with?"

"We're all at Betty Sue's – except for you. She called and suggested an impromptu dinner since Sharon was up visiting, and her 'sweetie' had an important business dinner somewhere."

Peg hoped they didn't hear her snort through the phone. "Ha! I could tell you all about that dinner...I wonder what Betty Sue would think of it?"

"I think that can wait a bit. But if you're not far off, come on by. The gang's all here, and Betty Sue just ordered enough Chinese Food to feed an army."

Peg drove the rest of the way thinking about questions she could ask her friend in order to obtain information. *He's up to no good, but if we stay one step ahead of him, we might be able to keep Betty Sue from getting hurt too badly.*

The gang's laughter greeted her through open windows when she pulled in. *Hell, I love these women. No matter what happens in life, we help each other through it – with a little wine, of course. And food. Real food—instead of bologna sandwiches.*

"You made it!" Betty Sue greeted her at the door. "I'm so glad you came – been awhile since the brunch club was *all* together."

"Well, you've been sort of busy with your new man. Surprised he hadn't claimed your weekend."

She gave Kelly a knowing look as she greeted the others and Betty Sue answered. "Oh, he was here early yesterday and stayed over. He had planned on staying the weekend, but while I was out this morning, he got a call from one of his potential investors and had to head off for a meeting shortly after I got back."

Jean brought Peg a glass of wine. "So, Betty, what does Sean do for a living? Sounds like he has a lot of meetings, but I don't recall you ever telling us."

Betty Sue retrieved her own glass and plopped down next to Arlene on the sofa. "My dear ladies, do you think I want to spend my time with my sweetie discussing boring things like jobs? Believe me, we've found much better ways to fill our days – and nights." She grinned at Arlene. "I don't want your pretty little church head to explode, but I gotta tell you ladies, I haven't had so much sex since I was in my 20s!"

"Oh, Jesus," Terri swore.

Arlene blushed. "I don't think we need those kinds of details."

Kelly shook her head. "Maybe *you* don't, but I'm sure curious. So, what's it like having all those orgasms at our age?"

Sharon almost spewed her wine all over the place, and Jean and Peg sat and grinned. Terri showed no emotion, as she had the best poker face of the group. Betty Sue, her faced flushed, stumbled over her words. "Oh, my Lord! I didn't say anything about *that*! After all, our bodies don't react quite the same as we get older. At least not us women – but sex is still wonderful knowing I've pleased my man."

Peg wasn't sure if Kelly was truly concerned or simply playing her friend, but she enjoyed the conversation nonetheless. "You mean to tell me that he hasn't satisfied you once in all your times together? Doesn't sound very gentleman-like to me."

If Betty Sue was annoyed, she hid it well. "Now, ladies, don't you worry your pretty little heads about my love life – I am doing fine in that area, okay? It's amazing to have a man back in my life who is so devoted. Any day now, I think he's gonna pop the question."

"What?!" Arlene replied. "So soon?"

"I believe so. After all, he told me he wanted to find a bigger place so my mother and Carla could come and stay if they needed to. Jean was there – ask her."

"Actually," Jean corrected, "we were talking about needing a place where Elena would have around the clock care, and Sean suggested a place large enough for all of you to live together."

Betty Sue rolled her eyes. "Well, that still sounds like his intentions are the same."

Peg munched on her egg roll in silence. *Oh, honey, if you only knew what his intentions are, or how devoted he actually is, you'd send him packing. And much as I'd love to blurt it all out right now, I wanna learn more about Tiffany Henderson. Tomorrow I'll need to meet up with Kelly, Sharon, Terri, and Jean to fill them in. Gonna be the greatest collaboration ever to take that cheating bastard down.*

As they all left later on that evening, Kelly sent a group message to everyone except Arlene and Betty Sue. "Tomorrow morning. My place at ten. Can you all make it?"

"*No way any of us won't be there,*" Peg texted back. "*You're all dying to hear what I discovered tonight. Be there – or you'll miss out!*"

Driving back down Stacey Boulevard toward home, she smiled as she passed by the fishermen's memorial, and then the widow's monument. *God, I love this town. Even though we lose men like Anthony to the sea while other scum bags like Sean McClean are abundant.*

Her house on Hesperus Ave. was less than half a mile from Hammond Castle. She'd inherited the house while her brother got the fishing boat. Peg might have joined them on the boat if females had been permitted, but instead she chose secretarial school. At age twenty, she landed a job at the Sentinel and worked her way up to one of the top journalist positions.

One of them. Never the top, though – the great stories, the ones that won awards, were always given to men – never me. At least my old boss gave me a few decent stories. Not anymore – not since the asshole editor arrived. Now it's charity events and local society crap. Such a waste of my abilities—all because I'm a woman.

She pulled in past the mailbox painted like a black cat, with the little flag for outgoing mail painted like one of the paws. Over the years she'd become the "crazy cat lady" in town, her house filled with cat paraphernalia and nine live felines – five black, four orange. *My babies. No one's ever loved me like they do.* The tattered cat flag flapped in the flower bed by the porch, and Franklin and Garfield, two orange tabbies, were lying in the front bay window.

Vinny was cleaning up the kitchen when she arrived home. "Hey, chicken stir-fry in the fridge if you're hungry."

Two black cats jumped up onto the counter and rubbed against her, demanding attention. "Hey Rosie, Midnight – you helping with the dishes? Where's the rest of you? And thanks, Vinnie, but I ate."

"Bologna sandwiches? Really?"

Loud purrs answered her loving scratches behind the ears. "Nawh, I ended up at Betty Sue's and she had Chinese take-out. Had a bowl of General Tso's chicken and rice, plus three different appetizers. Trust me, I'm stuffed."

Vinny dried his hands off. "You'll be hungry again in two hours. So, how was your stake out?"

"Awesome! Haven't had that much fun since I covered real news."

"I take it you got what you were looking for?"

"A solid start – but need to do a little research tonight. Tomorrow we're meeting up at Kelly's so I can fill them all in."

"But you were just at Betty Sue's – why didn't you spill it all then?"

Peg pulled out her laptop. "Not ready yet. We're checking up on her new boyfriend – and wanna make sure he doesn't screw Betty over."

"Find anything out?"

"Turns out the new beau isn't quite as faithful or honest as he pretends to be."

Vinny pulled up a chair. "I love a scandal! Hope sex is involved!"

Peg laughed. "Plenty of that going around, believe me."

Vinny watched her type and saw the name. "Wait! You're checking out Tiffany Henderson?"

"You know her? Rosie, not now...I need to work." The black cat continued purring, climbing up and draping herself around the back of her neck.

"She's a blogger —with quite a following. Type in 'Tiffany's Rants and Raves'. All about her latest recommendations and raves — both positive and negative. She hired me for a photo shoot a couple years back in Rockport. She's a bit of a diva, but nice enough. And she paid well, which is what I remember best!"

"I hear she has plenty to pay with?"

"Yeah, her dad was the founder of Henderson's Lawn Equipment. Left her without a care in the world when it comes to money and paying the bills. So how does she figure into all this?"

Peg grinned. "I was staking out Betty's new man, and guess who he's with right now?"

"No way! Tiffany and some old guy? That's just gross!"

"We sure don't see what the appeal is. I mean, he's getting laid any time he wants — and that seems to be frequently — but from what I hear his talent in bed isn't a huge selling point."

"Man, I gotta go with you to one of your dinners — you have way better conversations than we have here."

"I wouldn't doubt it. So, here's her blog...oh, and looky, looky. There's her new guy right now on her boat. Must have posted that tonight. Sean McClean, you're a bad boy!"

"Take a screen shot of that and save it. If he's trying to hide his tracks, he'll have her take that down."

"Unless she's not too bright when it comes to love. Don't forget, these ladies both think he's totally committed and loyal to them."

"But if there are incriminating photos of him online, he'll do whatever he has to in order to protect himself. Make sure the screen shot has the date of her post showing. Looks like some marina."

"It is — not far from her house in Salem. I ran in to Kelly's husband Travis while sitting out there."

"I *knew* I recognized it! Kelly had invited my mom for lunch one day to give her something, and I'd been out running errands with her, so she dragged me along. Pretty spot. So, you saw Travis?"

"Yep. Told him to fight for her – he still loves her, but might need to push her a bit."

"That doesn't always work, just sayin'."

Peg leaned back. "You're talking about your folks now, aren't you?"

"My mom, mostly. I'm not sure my dad will ever budge – but I can tell my mom wants to find some kind of connection. Just all that damn church guilt she's gotta work through. I tell ya, religion makes life so much more complicated than it needs to be."

"I won't argue with you on that. But faith gives a lot of us the inner strength we need to face each day – it's hard to reconcile that sometimes with rules we have a hard time with."

"I suppose."

"And it doesn't negate the importance of the faith – makes it harder, that's all. I suspect your dad struggles with you not being home, even if he doesn't talk about it."

"Not sure I agree with that, but I know you mean well."

Peg reached out and patted his arm. "Don't assume it can't happen. Even us stubborn Catholics can have epiphanies, you know." Turning back to her computer, she continued. "So, what else can you tell me about Tiffany? Has she dated over the years?"

"A few flings – nothing super serious. I doubt this Sean guy is anything more than another distraction. I don't think she ever lets anyone get too close."

"If my instincts are right, he only wants to get close to her money."

"And Betty Sue's as well?"

"Yep. And she's much more gullible, which is why we're all determined to expose him."

"Well, if you want me to dig, I'll be happy to help. In fact, I could drop her a line to ask about another photo shoot. She might love the opportunity, and I could do a little detective work of my own."

Peg stood up, and stretched as Rosie jumped down to the table. "Did I ever tell you how happy I am with you three kids staying here? You're all so damn talented."

Rosie meowed loudly and rubbed up against Peg once again. "Alright, alright! I get it – you guys are ready for dinner." She started picking up cat food dishes and counted various thumps from around the house. Around her feet, black and orange furballs gathered, insisting on supper as she tried to avoid tripping on them.

Vinnie laughed. "The only time when all nine are together. The black ones still confuse me – except Little Black Cat. She's so tiny compared to the others."

As he spoke, one black cat with a small white patch on her chest rubbed against his leg. "Oh, and Mitzi here. She's always the last to eat. Not sure if she's being polite or doesn't want the others around."

"Oh, it's the latter – she doesn't share her food. She has me trained to put a little dish up here on the counter, where the others won't dare jump up and mess with her." As she spoke, Mitzi did exactly what she predicted, and soon all nine cats were chowing down. "Sofia and Roberto both out tonight?"

Vinny nodded. "Roberto has a twelve-step meeting, and Sofia was meeting someone about doing their social media marketing – like she needs another client right now."

"Don't worry about her. For all she complains, she's thriving on all the work. Starting her own business took guts, and it's paying off big-time."

"I'll fill her in later tonight; I think she's done some work on Tiffany's website."

Peg reached down to pat two orange tabbies as they washed their faces. "Much appreciated. Think I'm gonna change into PJs before I do any more. If I miss you later, then sleep well."

"You, too – good luck with your digging."

Hours later, Peg closed down her laptop and scratched under Deacon's chin as he sprawled out over the items she'd printed out. "I'm gonna need all those, pal," she whispered. "May not be submissible in court, but it should convince the ladies he's an ass." She gathered a half dozen sheets of paper, two with photos of Tiffany and Sean, and the others involving the business and her father's obituary. There was also a list of places she'd donated generous checks to.

All Sean has to do is to come up with a business that helps people – she's all over those organizations. Wonder how much money she gives out each year? Gotta keep digging. But first, some sleep. A sleek black cat on the corner of her bed was the only one to greet her. "Hey Bagheera...you gonna come cuddle? The others are all conked out elsewhere." As she drifted off to sleep, she dreamed about stake outs and winning awards for journalism.

CHAPTER NINETEEN

Peg arrived at Kelly's with her tote bag, and after a mandatory greeting to Chianti, joined the others in the living room.

"I didn't invite Arlene today." Kelly began, "It might be wrong to exclude her, but she's not one to keep a secret, and we can't afford her slipping up and blurting something out. Last night, before Peg joined us at Betty Sue's, she followed our buddy Sean McClean around. Can't wait to find out what she discovered."

"I hardly slept after his surprise visit yesterday," Sharon said. "I hope you found some real dirt."

Peg placed her laptop on the coffee table. "I have all I need to prove he's a scum bag – but nothing to nail him on yet. So, here's the run down. When Sean left the townhouse, he stopped at a seedy motel for about thirty minutes to shower and change. Then I tailed him to a house in Beverly, where he picked up a hot blonde. They drove to a local marina for a romantic dinner before boarding a sailboat for the night."

"He hasn't changed a bit," Sharon said.

"So, he left Betty Sue's bed to go screw another woman?" Terri asked. "What a major asshole."

"For cheating on her, yes," Jean pointed out, "but if he has a nice boat, he might not be after her money at all."

Peg laughed as she pulled a folder out of her bag. "You're always the optimist. But the boat belongs to the blonde." She placed two photos on the table. "Meet Tiffany Henderson. Inherited it from her dad about six months ago – along with a hefty bank account."

"Breakfast at Tiffany's," Sharon read as she picked up a photo. "That's one hell of a boat. So, our suspicions are right after all."

"Even worse," Terri replied. "He's dating *two* rich women."

Everyone agreed except Kelly, who was studying the other photo. "This is Harbor Side."

Peg nodded. "Figured you'd recognize it. I...ah...ran into Travis while I was there."

"You didn't mention that in your text."

"Wasn't relevant. But he did ask about you – wanted to know how you were doing."

Kelly passed the photo on to Jean. "I hope you told him I was just fine."

"I told him what he needed to hear – I'll play the conversation for you later on. Might be a little muffled, but you'll—"

"Wait, you *recorded* it?" Kelly scoffed.

"Will you relax? It was an accident, okay?"

"How the hell do you record someone by accident?"

"Look, I was using my portable voice recorder to take notes and Travis startled me. The damn thing fell into my bra and I couldn't turn it off, okay?"

Laughter erupted from everyone. "I guess that explains why it's muffled," Terri said. "Bet you couldn't even swear with Travis right there."

Jean held up the photo of Sean and Tiffany having dinner. "I'm pretty sure Hannah showed me a video of her on YouTube."

"Has a blog, too. 'Tiffany's Rants and Raves.' Does reviews and recommendations about everything on Cape Ann."

"Yeah!" Jean answered. "She was on raving about some art show on Rocky Neck last year – and then ranting about the chowder she got for lunch afterwards."

Kelly giggled. "I wonder if she'll be ranting or raving about Sean this morning? I mean, what the hell does she see in him?"

"He can be a charmer at first," Sharon began. "Trust me, I know. The bigger question is what the hell is he up to?"

Peg held up the other papers from her folder. "He's probably aware of how generous she is with her money. Donates to lots of businesses and charities on Cape Ann."

Kelly perused the list. "North Shore Lab Rescues, Endowment for Starving Artist Relief, McQuaid's Fishermen's Aid, Stone Hill Foundation—"

Sharon interrupted. "Did you say "McQuaid?""

"Yeah – McQuaid's Fishermen's Aid. Why?"

"It may be a coincidence, but my husband's middle name was McQuaid."

"And Sean was your husband's business partner?" Terri asked. "Cause that don't sound like no coincidence."

Sharon joined Peg on the couch as the latter typed. "Here's their website. Says they do construction and storm repairs for fishermen short on funds. There are a few testimonials with photos – all raving about how—"

"Holy shit!" Sharon grabbed the laptop from Peg, hands shaking as she stared at the testimonial in front of her. "Those are Steve's cousins -- and I *took* those photos! So, how the hell did Sean get them, and how did Steve have anything to do with this?"

"Did they have a side business?" Jean asked.

"No way. After Steve started drinking, they couldn't save their own. I had to work to put food on the table and pay the mortgage."

Peg's next idea spurned excitement. "What if Sean's smarter than we think, and *he* ran a side business by himself? Had a drunk partner who never noticed invoices paying out to a fake company? Might have been *him* who ran the company into the ground."

Sharon was livid. "I sold my house to pay off those debts! Now I could kill the bastard!"

"How about a little boat ride?" Jean offered. "You'd be amazed at how many people fall overboard and are never seen again. Ah, shit... Terri, I'm sorry...after Anthony, I should—"

"Don't worry about it," Terri assured. "He didn't exactly fall overboard. And hell, Sean might be good chum for the sharks. I'm a fisherman's wife – I could lure him down to the pier for a ride."

Peg joined in. "Yeah, and take him out about a mile before confronting him. Sharon could pull out a knife. Hell, he'd have a heart attack before she could cut an arm off."

"Ladies, get a grip!" Kelly ended the adventure. "Fun as that might be, we can't kill him, okay? No point in going to jail for that scumbag. Besides, I want *him* to be the one wearing an orange jumpsuit, not one of us."

Jean agreed. "And using company funds to pay out fake invoices is larceny, so let's do some digging. Sharon, do you still have paperwork from the business stashed away somewhere?"

"Yeah, in a storage unit in Caldwell. Tim advised me to hold on to it for—oh, crap! Tim and Maggie are planning to celebrate their anniversary at the townhouse next weekend. What if Sean is next door at Betty Sue's?"

Kelly had the perfect suggestion. "She might love a girls' trip somewhere. We've taken lots over the years—had some great times, I might add."

"Damn right we did," Peg said.

Sharon grabbed her phone. "I can't guarantee she has a room, but my neighbor runs a bed and breakfast right in Caldwell. It would be awesome to show you guys around town—and foliage will be at peak next weekend."

Terri wasn't convinced. "Will she go, with her hot and heavy romance going on?"

"She won't refuse an early birthday present—on the only weekend I could grab." Kelly turned to Sharon. "Go on. Call her."

Within minutes, Sharon hung up smiling. "Barb – she's the owner – had a cancellation. I booked the last two rooms."

Kelly grabbed her phone. "Let me call Betty Sue and set this plan in motion. If anyone can take this bastard down, it's the brunch club!"

CHAPTER TWENTY

Elena was getting worse.

Hannah started every morning at Elena's day program talking about the weather and reminiscing on various topics related to the seasons. At times Elena couldn't recall Betty Sue's name, but would remember picking Carla up after school each day. But today, she had spoken instead about picking up Charlie.

"Who's Charlie, Elena?"

"Charlie – my little sister—she'd rather be my little brother, and go and fish with Papa, but he says girls don't belong on the boat. Poor Charlie. I need to pick her up and make her dinner."

"You cook for Charlie every day?"

"On school days, while Mama's at work. Everybody's gotta pitch in."

Rather than try to correct her, Hannah invited others to share their stories of pitching in as kids, and soon the room was full of laughter as each shared vivid memories of childhood. They still made her smile hours later as she prepared lunch in the kitchen.

"Someone's lost in their own little world," came a familiar voice. She looked up to find JJ standing in the doorway, leaning against the door jam. "I said hello and you didn't flinch."

Hannah smiled. "Sorry. Was thinking about Elena and how fast her dementia's progressing. Weird how it drags on forever in some people, but not her. I'm not sure she'll be able to come here much longer."

"So how does that affect you? Does that mean you wouldn't come, either? Cause that would suck."

God, that smile. Do you have any idea how much I love that smile? "Possibly. I'm her day time caregiver, so if she ends up having to live somewhere else, I might have to find another job." She sliced the last loaf of bread as she continued. "I'd miss it here, though."

"Would you miss me, too?"

"Of course I would, mister…who would I have to rant all about tiny houses to?"

"I love how animated you are talking about tiny houses, but I thought we might try the opposite this weekend and tour a great big place for contrast."

"Big place? What did you have in mind?"

"If you're interested, I'd really like to tour the Beauport estate over on Eastern Point."

"I went on a class trip in fourth or fifth grade, but all I remember was a window with tons of amber colored glass bottles. Field trips shouldn't be wasted on school kids."

"Exactly! We need adult field trips! After talking to all the builders at the tiny house expo, I'm dying to explore more architecture. Beauport has like forty rooms and they're all totally different in design. I mean, how cool is that?"

Hannah laughed as she stirred the soup and then got bowls and spoons out of the cabinet. "Forty rooms? I guess that's about as big a contrast as you can get to a tiny house. I'm not even sure Hammond Castle has forty rooms."

"Another place on my list! But do you wanna go on Saturday? My treat."

Hannah smiled, nodding shyly. "I'd like that. And I'm glad your folks are giving you a little more freedom."

"Every bit helps keep me sane. I'll pick you up around eleven. We can grab some lunch afterwards, and you can tell me how tiny houses are ten times better."

"Well, at least ten times smaller," Hannah kidded. "But yeah, eleven works. See you then."

The sounds of laughter and chatter drifted down the hall as Hannah placed the bread baskets on the table. As Elena and the others arrived to eat, she served them each a bowl of soup. *God help me. I better talk to Carla before Saturday; I don't want her thinking I'm going around behind her back, trying to steal the guy she wants. I can't help it if he's interested.*

She found Carla in the kitchen when she brought Elena back after day program ended. "You're home early."

"It was dead this afternoon. Joey told me to take off early." Carla greeted her grandmother with a warm hug. "Nonna, would you like to watch your game show until dinner's ready?"

"That would be lovely. I hope Alan Ludden is on today."

"Yup, Password starts in a few minutes. You get comfy in your rocker and I'll bring you some lemonade." As she grabbed a glass, she continued her conversation with Hannah. "How's she been today?"

"Not great. She was talking about having to fetch Charlie again. As the day went on, she got better, but mornings are tough."

"And getting worse. It sucks that I'm gonna be a complete stranger to her before too long." She brought the lemonade into the living room and placed it on the table. Elena was fidgeting with the buttons on her cardigan, buttoning and un-buttoning the same two. "Here you go, Nonna. You enjoy Password and I'm going to make us some ziti with meatballs for dinner, okay?"

Elena grabbed Carla's hand. "You're my best girl, Carla. You take good care of your Nonna."

Carla kissed Elena's forehead and squeezed her hand. "Just like you took care of me all these years. Love you, Nonna."

She returned to the kitchen with misty eyes. "And every now and then, she's clear as a bell – almost makes it harder."

"Yeah; you never know which Elena you'll deal with. So, have you talked to your mom about plans yet? Time's running out."

"I don't know why the hell she has to be here. She'll butt in through the whole meeting, trying to convince the lawyer how her ideas are what Nonna needs. She doesn't know shit."

"She *has* to be here – please tell me you invited her."

"Calm down – she's coming. But I don't have to like it."

Hannah grinned. "Fair enough. Did you call Jim Winston?"

"Yeah; he's coming in a couple of weeks; I hope he can tell us what she's done. She sure won't remember."

"No doubt."

Carla put a pot of water on the stove. "By the way, I told your mom about a tin box Nonna keeps under her bed. I checked, and nothing's in it about the house or a will or anything."

"Maybe the lawyer has it. I could keep Elena company while he's here so you guys can work without interruptions."

"Thanks. I'll text you the details. I tell ya, it was hard finding a night when he was free and Mom and I weren't out on dates."

Hannah took a step backwards, noting Carla's softer demeanor for the first time. *Crap! Has she gone out with JJ? He didn't say anything about it.* "A date? Start talkin', missy."

Carla grinned. "Hey, it's nothing compared to Mom's hot and heavy romance, but I met a guy at work– new in town – and we've been out twice already. And get this -- I haven't even slept with him yet."

Hannah chuckled. "Well, that's progress – I'm happy for you."

"Thanks. And pardon me if I don't introduce you quite yet – I don't need another guy telling me he's into someone else and know that it's you."

"What are you talking about?"

"Oh, don't play innocent with me," Carla chided. "I talked to JJ and tried to line up a night out, but he said he was interested in someone and didn't want to date anyone else until that option was shut down. Doesn't take a genius to know who the hell he's talking about."

Hannah felt her face flush. Carla must have noticed, because the pasta stopped mid-air instead of being poured into the pot of boiling water. "So has he asked you out yet?"

Before Hannah could come up with an excuse, or justification, Carla uttered the words she thought she'd never hear. "Look, I've always told you JJ was off limits, but he's obviously into you; doesn't seem fair to guilt you into not responding. Guess I was being a selfish brat of a friend, huh?"

Hannah gave her a little hug. "How 'bout an insecure friend – and it sounds like this new guy might be building your confidence a bit. But thanks for letting me know."

"So, has he? Asked you out?"

Hannah nodded. "This morning, actually. Wants me to go and tour the Beauport museum with him on Saturday."

"A museum? JJ? Maybe it's just as well I gave up on him. That sure ain't my style." She took a few leftover meatballs from the fridge and put them in a pot with a jar of sauce. "So, you going?"

"I guess I am now. The museum sounds kinda cool."

"Nerds ... the two of ya – except he doesn't look like one."

"Speaking of which, what does this new guy look like? And does he have a name?"

"Paul. He moved down from Maine last month and is working on the docks, and he knows the lobster business pretty well. Came in for a drink one night and sat at the bar talking till we closed."

"And since then?"

Carla grinned. "He's been in several nights a week and does the same thing – sits at the bar and chats. A couple of times he came in with some locals and shot a few games of pool, but I think he's interested. Guess we'll find out."

"He better treat you well, or I'll have to track him down and have a little chat."

"Yeah, you'll do no such thing – I won't even let you meet him till things are more secure, got it?"

"You bet. I'll go and bring Elena in for dinner. You're such a good person, Carla. You really are."

"Oh, don't get all lovey-dovey with me – makes me ill. You want some of this?"

Hannah shook her head as she headed into the living room. "Nope. Going over to eat with my mom tonight. But thanks!"

Once Elena was eating, Hannah said her goodbyes and walked across the street, smiling with anticipation for her date with JJ. *It'll be so nice if this new guy works out for Carla – and maybe I can finally explore a relationship with JJ without feeling guilty.*

CHAPTER TWENTY-ONE

Tuesday morning Kelly was at work posting new homes for sale when the call arrived.

"I sure hope the most beautiful realtor on Cape Ann remembers me. This is Sean McClean – Betty Sue's favorite guy?"

Despite wanting to gag over the saccharine tone, Kelly responded in her most professional voice. "Of *course*, I remember you. I must admit, I was beginning to wonder if Betty Sue had been exaggerating about your interest in looking at houses. Sometimes she can be a little idealistic about things."

Even Sean's laugh was forced. "Aw...now that's one of the things I love most about my sugar – she always finds the bright side to every little thing. I can't tell you how mighty blessed I am to have found such an amazing lady."

Yeah, an amazingly rich lady, you skunk. To go along with the other rich chick you're banging. "I think all of us agree you're damn lucky to be dating Betty Sue. Someday you'll have to tell us more about how you two got together – but this morning, I'm assuming you're calling about houses."

"I am indeed. I'd like you to help me find the perfect house for my sugar and me. Her birthday's coming up, and I wanna surprise her with a love nest."

"I think the first step is to meet and find out what you're looking for," Kelly replied. "That helps me to narrow down the search—"

"I'm ahead of ya. I have two spots all picked out for you to set up showings."

"I like a client who does their homework."

"So, you gonna share the commission, then?" Sean laughed. "Only kidding, beautiful. I'm sure you're worth every penny of what I'll be paying you."

Kelly fought the urge to tell him off. "Why don't you give me the addresses and I'll set up the showings. Either Tuesday or Wednesday next week?"

"Sure thing. I'm busy, but flexible."

Kelly was familiar with both properties as she scribbled the addresses down. "Both of these are out on Eastern Point-- with some hefty price tags. I could show you some lovely homes farther inland that wouldn't—"

"Not to worry, beautiful. I've been rather successful with my latest investments."

You mean the two rich ladies you're two-timing? "Gee, I should ask for *your* card when we meet. I could use an investment professional myself."

Sean's voice brightened, not recognizing the sarcasm. "You don't say? I guess a realtor in this area makes great dough. Beautiful *and* smart; I like that in a woman."

Are you seriously hitting on me? Even though you're screwing one of my closest friends? And do I dare try to lead you on a bit to prove what a complete ass you are? "I can understand why Betty Sue brags about you so much."

Sean took the bait. "My sugar brags about me? You'll have to fill me in on all the good stuff she has to say."

"As Betty Sue's friend, I think I'd best keep quiet about what she tells me."

"A secret, huh?" Sean snorted. "Damn, she must be bragging about how good I am in bed."

God, you make my skin crawl. "Um, maybe we should stick to real estate," Kelly uttered.

"Hey, I'm just yanking your chain, beautiful. A little teasing between friends. I sure hope I didn't offend you."

"None taken, Sean. Can I have your number, and I'll call you with details?"

"Perfect. I can't wait to take a look. And don't forget, not a word to my sugar. I wanna surprise her with the perfect place – and I'll rely on your input. Talk to you soon!"

Kelly brought up the first house. *What an ass! Let's see what you're looking at. Okay, three bedrooms, so Elena and Carla—wait a minute! Why the hell do you need a deep-water dock? You don't own a boat; but Tiffany does!* "Not on my watch, pal. No way you're buying her a house with my friend's money, you bastard."

She set up showings for the following week and called both Jean and Peg to fill them in, and then Sharon in Caldwell. "Hey, it's Kelly. Got a minute?"

"Sure. What's up?"

"Any chance you can be late to work tomorrow? It has to do with Operation Sean Be Gone."

"In that case, you've got my full attention."

"Can we get into your storage unit first thing? I want those bins from Steve's office. My gut's telling me those files have the evidence we need."

Sharon winced. "Did anything happen up there? You're making this sound kind of urgent."

"Sean called me this morning. He wants to buy a house. An expensive waterfront place. Most likely with Betty Sue's money."

"That scumbag!" Sharon hissed. "We can't let that happen."

"And we won't. But we need something tangible to nail him, and Peg and Jean agreed to help me look through those files. If I can come down first thing to grab them, we might have something to celebrate when we all arrive this weekend."

Sharon smiled. "Nothing in the world would make me happier. Hey, I gotta run. A truck just pulled in with a delivery I have to help unload.

Call me when you're on your way tomorrow and I'll give you directions."

"Will do. And Sharon?"

"Yeah?"

"I'm so glad you showed up in Gloucester. Betty Sue would be so screwed if you hadn't been here to meet Sean."

"I'll do everything I can to help protect her."

"You're a real friend, lady – see you in the morning."

Sharon hung up and waved as the driver opened the back of the delivery truck. *They have become friends, haven't they? First, I get my family back. And now I have some wonderful friends. And I'll be damned if Sean McClean thinks he can screw that up.*

* * *

Sharon stopped by the storage unit after work, grimacing as the mechanical door rumbled up to allow access. *I haven't been here since I moved back to Caldwell. Why the hell am I paying money to keep all this stuff?* Half of the small unit held sentimental items from her house in Maine, and the other half contained remnants from Steve's office. She found the boxes marked "financial files" along one wall as she'd been diligent in packing them.

Piled next to those were a number of unmarked bins. *All of Sean's crap. I should have thrown it all away—exactly what I told him when he called ranting about his personal items. Is there something in this mess he didn't want anyone to find?*

With resolve, she opened the first few bins, rifling through folded up blueprints, take out menus, mugs, office supplies, and closed client files. *Jesus, this is all useless crap; I need to purge every piece of Sean McClean left in here. His negative energy seeps out of every box I open.*

Frustration mounted as she tackled the last bin, but at last she unearthed an old paper ream box with "charities" scrawled on the top corner. Inside, numerous file folders and manila envelopes covered a small book underneath. *A ledger? Is this the item you were ranting about?* Scanning through the pages, her heart skipped a beat when she found several marked "McQuaid Fishermen Relief." *Oh, my God. This has to be it!* With shaking hands, she found the corresponding manila envelope, and fumbled with the metal fastener to dump the papers out. With heart racing, she scanned through the pile. *Business certificates with Sean's name, doing business as McQuaid's Fishermen Relief. Why four different towns?* Each listed construction, architectural consults, and boat repairs as the activities. *I'm sure this is what you were ranting about. There has to be something illegal here, and we're gonna nail you, you bastard!* She tucked everything back into the box and placed it on top of the marked financial boxes. *I can't wait for Kelly's arrival tomorrow.*

CHAPTER TWENTY-TWO

Kelly arrived before 8:00 the next morning, and Sharon was waiting at the storage unit when she pulled in. "Man, you really are an early riser!"

"Wanted to beat the traffic – we both know what a nightmare 128 can be at rush hour. Great directions, by the way. And you sure sounded chipper this morning."

Sharon grinned as she unlocked and rolled up the door. "Well, I stopped by after work yesterday and found something you might be able to use." She led Kelly to the back of the unit and handed her the box she'd gone through the previous night.

"Computer paper?" Kelly asked. When Sharon tapped on the top corner, she held up the box to read the scrawled writing. "Charities? Can we take a peek now?"

"I found McQuaid's Fishermen Relief – and several others." Sharon's voice bubbled with excitement. "And underneath you'll find a small ledger."

Kelly placed the box on the desk as she rifled under the files to pull out the book. "I do believe this is something concrete to work with," she said, skimming through the pages. "And it looks like there are at least three other accounts here besides the McQuaid one."

Sharon nodded. "A manila envelope for each of them, although I only opened the McQuaid one."

"Find anything?"

"Oh, yeah...several business certificates with Sean's signature notarized – all started five years ago. And the McQuaid envelope had those photos we saw on his website."

"Hell, yeah!" Kelly exclaimed. "If those are fake, then I suspect the others are, too!"

"Let's hope so. The financial files were easy to find – I was sure to label them while packing. I'll help you carry them out to the car." As they each grabbed a box, she continued. "Tim helped to pack these separately, knowing we'd need to hold on to them for a number of years in case anything came back to bite us after the business was dissolved."

They unloaded the first bins into Kelly's trunk and returned for the other two. Kelly opened one bin and carefully placed the cardboard box on top of the other boxes inside. "Don't want anything to damage this baby. You do realize we might have everything we need to land that asshole in jail?"

Sharon gazed over at the other bins she'd opened the night before. "I went through all those last night – mostly Sean's personal crap. I don't think anything else in them is useful, but we can always make a quick stop here over the weekend if needed. Quite honestly, I could have easily missed that box entirely."

"I can't believe he didn't think to take it with him when he left."

"Last night I remembered a phone call I'd gotten from him," Sharon explained as she closed and locked the unit. "He was ranting about wanting some personal items from the office, and I told him we threw all his stuff away. I guess he figured we had, or he would have been hounding Tim when they worked on the hardware store debacle."

"He'd probably shit in his pants if he knew the box still existed – and that we're gonna analyze every piece of paper in the next couple of days."

Sharon leaned against Kelly's car. "You have no idea how much I wanna be up there with you today."

"You *could* follow me up."

"I thought about it, believe me, but I didn't want my workload result in someone having to work overtime. Besides, it might come back to bite me with overtime this weekend, and I am *not* giving up my time with all of you here in Caldwell."

"We're all getting stoked. Even Betty Sue is excited about her birthday weekend away. I spotted the Bed & Breakfast on my way into town – looks adorable."

"My friend Barb is looking forward to having you guys here – and even my dad is excited to meet all of you."

"Speaking of which," Kelly said, reaching into the car to grab her purse, "I have those keys for you to give to your son Tim. The old ones won't work anymore."

Sharon took the separate key rings. "Three sets?"

"Four, actually. One for you, Tim, and Maggie – and I have one I'll keep for Carla."

"Won't Betty Sue be suspicious that she doesn't have a set?"

Kelly chuckled. "I can string her along for a bit – at least until this guy's arrested."

"I'm more concerned he might try stopping by the townhouse this weekend. I would hate for him to run into Tim and Maggie."

"Not to worry; Peg's as excited about following him around as we are to visit Caldwell."

Kelly's tone softened. "I do feel bad for Betty. She has no idea what's coming."

"After this weekend, we'll have to tell her, won't we?"

"Not necessarily," Kelly replied. "If we find real evidence of a crime, we may be able to hand it over to the police and blame it all on karma." She stifled a yawn. "I better start back. Where can I grab a cup of coffee for the ride?"

"Best coffee shop in town is right by my house and the Bed and Breakfast. And be sure to grab a breakfast sandwich or a baked good as well. They're all made by a young guy named Brian, who made Tim and Maggie's wedding cake. Tell him I sent you and said hi. I'll bring all of you over to meet him this weekend."

"Wanna join me for a quick cup?"

Sharon shook her head. "I need to be at work by nine. If you follow me back into town, I'll drive past the shop so you can find it. You'll see the Bed & Breakfast up on the corner; turn right and you'll be back on your way."

"Sounds good," Kelly said getting into her car. "And I promise I'll call later with an update on the stash in my trunk."

"I'm counting on it, believe me. Safe travels."

She made sure Kelly was behind her as she passed by the diner and headed into town, and beeped as Kelly waved out the window when they reached the cafe. *Can't wait to show them around. We may not have the salt air or the ocean, but I think they'll love this little town as much as I do.*

CHAPTER TWENTY-THREE

Several hours later, Kelly anticipated the arrival of several from the brunch club. She'd placed one bin by each chair in her dining room, ensuring that Sean's "charity" box was at her spot. Chianti's bark alerted her before the doorbell rang. Kelly greeted Jean and Terri at the door as Peg pulled in. "Nothing like friends who all arrive on time. Come on in."

"We're all motivated to nail this bastard," Peg said, huffing a bit as she climbed the stairs. "I've got a good feeling about today."

"Wait till I show you what Sharon dug up last night," Kelly placed the envelopes and ledger on the table. "This pile right here might be all we need. Turns out Sean has several side businesses, all of which are included in the ledger. Had them stashed in a cardboard box."

"How the hell did Sharon end up with it?" Jean asked.

"She was stuck cleaning out the office; packed everything up and put it in storage. I guess he called once ranting about some personal possessions, but she told him everything had been thrown out."

"And after all these years," Jean offered, "He figured he was in the clear."

"He'd go ballistic if he knew we had 'em." Peg gestured toward the pile. "So, when do we get to take a peek?"

Kelly passed the ledger to Terri. "I'll put you in charge of the book, and each of us can have an envelope. I have McQuaid's Fishermen Relief, which Sharon glanced through. The photos of Steve's cousins are here, so he definitely used fake information on the website."

"Still gotta prove he did it," Peg cautioned.

"Agreed," Jean said. "And we're only gonna have one shot to take this guy down."

"Yeah, and even then, what do we do?" Terri asked. "Walk into the police station and drop everything on their desks? They'll write us off as middle-aged crones playing Nancy Drew."

Peg's deep laugh was contagious. "Don't worry, ladies. Sofia, one of my boarders--her brother is a detective, and she'll call him as soon as we find something."

"Is there anyone you *don't* know in this city?" Kelly teased. She held up the business certificates from her envelope. "Hopefully these will help. Sean has a business license from four different towns for his little McQuaid side business."

"Why separate ones for each place?"

"Those are DBA forms," Peg cut in, "Doing business as a self-run company. Allows the owner to set up a bank account with the business name, but write checks personally. Sean's smarter than we think."

"She's right," Kelly continued. "Less paperwork and filing with various state agencies. So, all of these list construction and boat repair as the main activities."

Peg had opened hers. "I've got North Shore Handyman here – with DBA certificates for five different towns. Damn, that's almost every coastal town on the North Shore."

Jean squinted to read the faded words scrawled in the corner of her item. "This one says 'SURFS.' What the hell does that stand for?"

"There's an account in the ledger for Stevenson's Urgent Recovery From Storms. Let's see what's inside."

Jean spilled the contents of her envelope on the table, finding four more notarized certificates. "These cover the coast south of Salem... he's got everything from Boston to NH."

Peg scanned all the papers on the table. "So, what the hell do they mean?"

Terri held up the ledger. "These accounts only list dates with deposits and withdrawals. No notes or line items about the money going in or out. Sounds fishy."

Jean stuffed her papers back into the envelope and reached for a bin. "What if he was taking money out of the real business by making payments to all these fake ones. Wouldn't those show up somewhere in the files?"

"Ding! Ding!" Kelly said. "Don't you see? If we can find a bunch of payments made out from Steve and Sean's business that match up to some of these accounts, we'll have enough of a paper trail to call Sofia's detective brother."

Terri continued scanning through Sean's secret ledger book. "So where are the ledgers from Sean and Steve's business? Can't make a connection without 'em."

Kelly perused her pile. "They're on computer print outs. Each year has its own folder."

Excitement grew as the ladies narrowed down their search and found the corresponding folders from each bin. Jean readjusted her reading glasses. "Terri, why don't you stick with the ledger, and give us the first five dates that a deposit was made? All of us can search through to see if anything around that date matches something paid out. Does that make sense?"

Peg scribbled down the dates Terri read out and opened her first file. "I can't remember the last time I was so excited about a job!" For several minutes they worked silently, each poring through receipts and monthly bank statements. Kelly was the first to break the silence. "Bingo!" she exclaimed, holding up a simple lined sheet with "contractor invoice" written in bold letters. "Here's one for North Shore Handyman for $3,000, marked paid on April 12th – lists floor installation, but no details."

Terri's smile confirmed what they all suspected. "Deposit made for $3,000 on April 13th. Is that enough to nail him?"

"Not yet," Peg warned. "It might prove the money was paid out, but it doesn't prove the work wasn't done or anything else, for that matter. But a bunch of those? All with vague work orders listed? It might be enough to convince the police to keep searching."

By the end of the afternoon, the needed stack of receipts had grown, all matching up with a deposit made to one of Sean's accounts. "So, what do we do now?" Jean asked.

Peg scrolled through her phone. "I'm gonna call Sofia for Juan's number. She told him a little about what's going on, and he was quite interested."

Jean chuckled. "I bet. Larceny isn't something the Gloucester force has to deal with on a regular basis."

Thirty minutes later, Peg said goodbye to Detective Juan Hernandez. "We all look forward to seeing you as well. And thanks, detective." She put her phone on the table. "He's coming tomorrow at 1:00 to pick up everything you have."

Kelly sat quietly, staring down at the pile of papers on her table. "I keep thinking about Betty Sue. She's gonna hate us for doing this. Nothing like whisking her away for a birthday weekend the day after you've given police evidence to arrest Sean."

"Hey, we're trying to *save* her from this guy, remember?" Jean said. "Besides, once we're in Caldwell, Sharon will keep us entertained. I'm looking forward to a weekend with the girls." She glanced toward Terri. "I wish you and Arlene were coming along, though."

Terri placed the ledger on top of the stack of receipts. "When Sean gets arrested, we can have a celebration together."

Peg shook her head. "I doubt Betty Sue will be up to partying then. But we can all be there for her until the next man comes along. Let's face it; she's never alone for long."

"I guess you're right," Kelly replied. "In the meantime, I'll call Sharon to fill her in after you guys take off."

By the end of the afternoon, Kelly had stacked all the bins for the detective when her phone rang. *Travis.* Her heart raced as the third ring began. *Do I dare?*

Taking a deep breath, she hit the green button. "Hello."

There was a pause on the other end. "Kelly? It's...me. Travis."

As countless memories of his voice, his arms around her, and then his face as she walked out of her birthday party came flooding back, Kelly leaned against the counter for support. *Remember what Sharon said about the abyss. Don't let it grow deeper and wider.*

"It's...been awhile." She tried to swallow, her mouth dry and her tongue like sandpaper.

A longer pause. "I wasn't sure if you'd answer."

"I guess that makes two of us, to be honest."

"I'm glad you did. I've picked up the phone a hundred times, but never got the nerve."

I know exactly what you mean. "So, what changed this time?"

"I...um...I ran into Peg at the marina awhile back, and you've been on my mind ever since. Figured I had nothing left to lose by calling – but maybe something to gain?"

I can tell you're hurting, too. Can hear it in your voice.

"Kelly? You still there?"

Blinking back tears, Kelly answered, her voice almost a whisper. "I'm here." *Please ask, Travis – I don't think I have the strength myself.*

"I was hoping we...look, if you still hate me, I'll understand. But...if we could at least meet for coffee. I can't give up without attempting to try and fix it. Please. Just coffee."

As if I've ever hated you – even when I wanted to. Kelly's hands trembled as she took Sharon's advice. "Okay. I can do coffee." *There, I've jumped. Please, Travis, don't let me fall.*

CHAPTER TWENTY-FOUR

Even along the back roads, the twenty-minute ride to Manchester-By-the-Sea seemed endless. Kelly had suggested a small breakfast café halfway between the condo and the marina. *As if location is going to keep the memories away, but down here is a little more neutral, I guess. God, help me breathe.*

He was sitting in a booth by the front window when she walked in, giving a slight wave and a timid smile. *Just keep your cool, and try to limit the knee-jerk reactions.* "Morning." She slid in across from him and tried to relax the knot in between her shoulders. "Been here long?"

"A few minutes. I wasn't sure how busy it might be, so I came early to grab a spot. The waitress brought our water and the menus, and—" He paused, fumbling with the corner of the menu in front of him. "You look great, by the way…"

She met his gaze for a moment, noting his black curls and a deep tan from summer months on the boat which made his eyes bluer and his smile whiter. "You as well. Your tan puts mine to shame."

Travis chuckled. "I guess living on a boat all summer does that – but the Labor Day fishing trip helped for sure."

"Of course; how are the guys?" For as long as Kelly had known

Travis, he'd headed off with his two best friends for an annual Labor Day fishing trip up the coast.

"Jack and Loni are expecting again – a girl this time – and CJ finally got engaged."

"Same girl he was dating?"

The waitress arrived before Travis answered, and they both ordered coffee. "No, they broke up shortly after...we did. He met Gina last summer and said he knew the first week that she was the one. They're getting married in the spring. You'd like her, I think."

"I'm happy for him. I never liked Trisha; she always corrected him whenever we went out." Picking up her menu, Kelly continued. "I guess we should decide what we want before she comes back, huh?" *Not that I have to think about it; I have the cranberry-orange scone every time I come here. And you'll no doubt order the western omelet, because you always do.*

After proving her intuition correct, he handed the menus to the waitress. "How about you? Anything new with the gang?"

"Where to start?" Kelly asked, sipping her coffee before answering. "Right now, we're all working on catching a con man before he gets his hands on Betty Sue's money."

"And here I was expecting updates to Terri's sciatica and Arlene's latest knitting project. But a con man? For real?"

"Sure looks that way. We're actually meeting with a Gloucester detective this afternoon."

"Jesus, you must have a real case! What the hell happened?" Excitement turned to doubt. "That is, if you're willing to share..."

"Hopefully you'll be reading about it in the paper before long," Kelly filled Travis in on the events of the past month, and as she was finishing up, the waitress approached with their food.

Travis took a big bite of his omelet. "Now it makes sense as to why Peg was sitting at the marina. I've seen the guy on many occasions with Tiffany. Some of the regulars wonder what the hell she sees in him when she won't give them the time of day."

"Yeah, I guess money and looks would be pretty attractive to a lot of guys." *I wonder if you were one of them. Her boat's only a few slips aways, so I'm sure you've run into each other lots of times.*

"She could have her pick of several on any given weekend – and they'd all be decent to her – until they learned what a spoiled brat she is. You should hear how nasty she is to the waitresses sometimes."

I guess that answers my question. God, I wish my brain didn't automatically go into suspicion mode with you.

"At any rate, I'm glad Peg was there that day...she's...kinda the reason I got up the nerve to call." Travis' voice dropped to a whisper. "I'd give anything for a chance to try and fix things between us. I miss you so damn much."

Kelly swallowed hard, caught between longing and fear. *You'll never find out if you don't try. You know you still love him.*

With tears in her eyes, she met his gaze. "I...miss you, too," she choked out. As Travis reached out and covered her hand with his, a jolt of energy surged through her, giving life to her indecision. For the first time since he'd left, she welcomed his soft touch and gently squeezed his thumb. "I've done lots of thinking, and I guess I owe you—or us—at least a chance."

Travis wiped his eyes with his free hand. "God, I've waited so long to hear those words...and I'll do anything, Kelly – you name it, I'll do it. We were too good together not to fight to have it back."

Kelly nodded, unable to speak. *Breathe...don't forget to breathe. You've met him halfway, so be willing to let him in. You can't learn to trust him again if you don't let him in.* "How about starting with a hike next weekend? I'm away with the girls this week."

"You up for a day at Halibut Point? Unless you'd prefer a place more neutral—"

"No, the point would be perfect," Kelly replied. "I'll bring Chianti along if that's okay."

"Please do; I've missed that little furball."

"I'm sorry I didn't let you see him when we split; that wasn't fair to either of you."

"It's okay; I understand. But thanks for offering to bring him along."

Kelly's phone interrupted them with an incoming text. "I better check that," she said. "It might be Sofia or her brother."

Travis let go of her hand. "Take all the time you need. I'm not going anywhere."

God, I hope you're right. Because I don't think I could bear to lose you a second time.

* * *

Several hours later, Kelly said goodbye to Detective Juan Hernandez after all the bins had been turned over. She rejoined the others in the living room, flopping down on the couch as she kicked off her shoes. "I guess now we wait."

"Not too long, I hope," Jean said. "Gonna be weird spending the weekend with Betty Sue all the while wondering if an arrest is imminent."

Terri grunted as she stood up, rubbing her hip and butt. "I can't sit anymore; this damn sciatica is killing me."

"Sorry," Kelly offered. "I should have offered you the firmer chair."

"Hell, it ain't the furniture – damn old age catching up, that's all. And I guess you'll have the toughest time this weekend since you'll be rooming with her."

"That reminds me!" Kelly exclaimed. "I have to call her sweetie before we head to Caldwell this weekend. I have a showing scheduled for next Tuesday."

Peg grinned. "You gonna ask him to measure Tiffany's boat to make sure the docks are big enough? I'll bring along my tape measure when I tail him this weekend."

Terri almost choked on her drink as she pulled a dining room chair over to sit in. "God, I'd love to see the look on his face if you did."

"Let's not lose focus, ladies," Kelly reminded. "Hard as it is, we simply have to play nice for a while—but man, I'll need every ounce of self-control not to taunt him next week."

"You should call Detective Hernandez and give him the address of that showing," Jean suggested. "You know, in case he might want to stop by and show Sean an arrest warrant."

Peg agreed. "Can't happen soon enough, for Betty Sue's sake. Still,

I'm gonna enjoy every minute of tailing that skunk until he's behind bars. Even another boring weekend sitting alone at the marina."

"You could always hang out with Travis." All conversation stopped with Kelly's statement. Her cheeks flushed as she became the focal point in the room. "I...met him for breakfast this morning."

"Hallelujah!" Jean responded. "You did the right thing, girlfriend. How'd it go?"

"I was nervous as hell, but God, it was good to talk. I suggested a hike for next week, and we're gonna take it slow." She glanced at Peg. "I guess I have you to thank. He told me about your little chat when you were at the marina last time."

"Hell, I gave him a nudge. You two belong together. All of us want you to be happy."

Kelly smiled at their assent. *I want that, too. And damn it, I want it with him. Thank God I have my friends to give me strength every step of the way—especially when my fears pop back up to block the way.*

CHAPTER TWENTY-FIVE

Sharon said goodbye to Tim and Maggie as they headed to Gloucester for the weekend, and then prepared for her friends to arrive. Carl complained in his good-natured way the entire time, following her into the kitchen with his crossword puzzle book while she cooked. "Why you making dinner for all of 'em with free meals at the Bed & Breakfast?"

Sharon grinned as she slid the roast chicken into the oven. "Because I'm excited to have my friends meet you. I've told them all about you, you know."

"Pfft. Don't expect me to entertain them. All that noise."

Sharon gave his shoulders a loving squeeze. "I promise they won't stay late, and you can escape to your room any time you want." *I know damn well you'll relish every bit of attention, and as long as no one mentions Sean McClean, we'll all have a great evening.*

When Jean's text announced they were only a couple of miles out of town, she kissed the top of Carl's bald head and promised she'd be back soon. "I'm heading over to Barb's to greet them and help them settle in, and then we'll be back. At least one of them is looking forward to seeing your roses."

Carl scowled. "I better go and find my sweater. I won't let strangers out there alone without supervision."

"Relax, Dad," Sharon assured as she headed out the door. The afternoon sun promised a warm walk through the park, and the orange and yellow maples were vibrant against the blue sky. *They might have the salt air up north, but I have the brighter foliage here.* By the time she arrived at Barb's Bed & Breakfast, Kelly's car turned the corner from Washington Street, and within minutes she was hugging each of them as they grabbed their overnight bags.

"Glad you found it," Sharon said. "Welcome to Caldwell — I can't wait to show you around!"

Jean stretched as she gazed at the park. "I'm already impressed. A park with a fountain and gazebo right outside our door?"

Sharon pointed across the lawn. "My house is the first one at the other end; I'll help you settle in, and then we can stroll down."

Barb opened the back door before they could head around to the front of the building. "So glad to finally meet you ladies! Come on in this way; and welcome to Caldwell!"

"This is my friend Barb," Sharon said as they made their way inside. "She and Scott run this place, and she also helped to start the community garden — which I'll show you in a bit. Sharon, these are some awesome ladies from Gloucester: Jean, Kelly, and Betty Sue, who owns the townhouse next to Tim."

Warm chatter filled the living area, and after pointing out the dining room, Barb led them upstairs. "Sharon told me you're eating over there tonight, but if you're hungry later, help yourself to the baked goodies on the kitchen table. Breakfast is anytime between seven and ten. You have these two rooms with a shared bath. I'll let you get settled, as another guest is pulling in."

She hustled back down the stairs as Jean peeked in each room. "Why don't you two take the bigger room," she said to Kelly and Betty Sue. "A twin bed is all I need."

Betty Sue smiled. "I'm glad you offered, 'cause I'm used to sprawling out when I sleep. Of course, I'll be lonely sleeping without my sugar bear to keep me warm."

"Aw, stop your pouting," Kelly teased. "Our goal is to have so much fun, you won't even miss him." She dropped her suitcase on the first bed. "You can have the bed next to the bathroom. Now let's get this party started, shall we?"

As they walked through the park, Sharon pointed out a pathway by the gazebo that led to a well-lit building through the trees. "That's our new community center -- the one Tim proposed and built." They reached the community garden that adjoined her dad's property. "A few ladies started this project with Barb a few years ago, and now every plot is full. I picked fresh veggies this morning for dinner tonight."

Jean spotted the old Victorian beyond. "Your dad's house is gorgeous, and I can smell his roses from here."

"We'll let him walk out to the garden with us," Sharon said. "He's a softie inside, but he's mighty protective of his roses. I planted most of them with my mom, and he tended to them the whole time I was gone. Come on in, and meet the old curmudgeon."

As expected, Carl's grumbling was all in jest, and he welcomed Kelly and Betty Sue on each arm as he showed off his backyard. Jean was brave enough to admire each rosebush up close, breathing in their sweet aroma. "Carl, your roses are stunning, and the colors complement one another so well. Are these Niagara?"

Carl's voice was warm with approval. "Ah, a lady who knows her roses? They are indeed – Rainbow Niagara, to be precise. Sharon picked those out as a little girl herself; liked the two-tone blend. Her mom Ruthie picked out the others, and they're all holding on all these years later."

"Only because he gave them so much love and care," Sharon boasted. "Would you ladies care for a glass of wine before dinner? I've got several bottles chilling inside."

"A perfect host!" Kelly exclaimed. "I'm sure ready for a glass after the drive. Carl, can we entice you to join us? I've heard that you are a master at crossword puzzles, and both Jean and I are willing to take you on if you're game."

The old man's step quickened. "You're on! I'll wait for dinner before any wine myself, though – gotta pace myself at my age. Sharon, you didn't tell me your friends were fellow puzzlers!"

Sharon held the door for Betty Sue as the others had gone in ahead of them. "I hope he doesn't bore you too much," she said.

"Don't you worry your pretty little head about that," her friend replied. "He's a charming old coot and I just adore him! Besides, he'll keep me from missing my man too much."

Sharon put her hand up. "Rule for the weekend," she cautioned. "This is a *girls'* weekend – no further mention of any men in our lives, okay?" *Please, dear God – especially no mention of that bastard.*

"Deal!" Betty Sue's laughter was light as she watched her friends settle down next to Carl and his puzzle. "With the exception of your dad, of course! And Sharon, your kitchen smells divine! I can't wait for a home-cooked meal with some of the best friends around."

* * *

Hours later, the ladies sat outside on the back patio, determined to finish off the second wine bottle. Kelly topped off everyone's before emptying the remnants into her glass. "Can't let good wine go to waste, can we?" She curled up next to Betty Sue on the glider and raised her glass. "Here's to great friends, and birthday celebrations that don't include calorie counting or portion control. We love our little Southern Belle – thank God you finally moved home."

Betty Sue laughed. "Even all those years living in Tennessee, you were still my besties – always will be. Nothing like friends who have your back no matter what."

Sharon shared the toast and gulped down some wine. *Shit, so why do I feel so guilty all of a sudden? Are you going to hate all of us next week?*

Jean offered reassurance. "Amen to that. Even when we piss each another off, we work through it. Always have, always will."

"And that goes for Peg, Terri, and Arlene, too," Kelly added. "To the brunch club – viva!" She reached over and squeezed Betty Sue's shoulder. "And a couple of weeks from now, we'll all have dinner for your actual birthday. Wish they were here now."

"Terri and Arlene both had to take care of their men," Betty Sue said, "but I was surprised that Peg couldn't join us."

Jean laughed. "Hell, she owns nine cats. That might be worse than a husband, come to think of it."

"Ah, ah, ah!" Kelly chided. "Girls' weekend – no chatting about men, remember?" Changing the subject, she turned toward Sharon. "So, what do you have planned for us this weekend? And it better include coffee at that little café you were telling me about."

Sharon chuckled. *Good thing you didn't reveal the fact you were there a few days ago buying your own. I hope Brian doesn't recognize you when we stop in.* "At some point, but tomorrow morning you'll be quite happy with the coffee that Barb serves with breakfast. And make sure you're up to eat, because her cooking is the bomb. Omelets with fresh veggies, home baked pastries, and all the bacon or sausage you can eat."

"Oh, Lord, I just gained five pounds thinking about it," Betty Sue chimed in. "But it will be worth it!"

"After you guys eat," Sharon continued, "I'll drive you around town to show you the highlights; it doesn't take long in a small town. Tomorrow afternoon I have us booked for a paint by wine class at the community center, and then dinner at the best Italian restaurant around."

Jean's ears perked up. "Is that a class where we paint and drink at the same time?"

"She's excited about the painting," Betty Sue pointed out. "The rest of us are much more interested in the wine part."

"Not only painting and drinking," Sharon countered, "But also a fundraiser for a local animal shelter. A young friend of mine adopted a shelter dog last year, and she's now done three of these classes to raise money for adoption events."

"Hell, if we're helping our furry friends, then sign me up," Kelly replied. "What a neat idea."

Jean nodded. "Absolutely. I've considered teaching some wine and paint classes, and I could contact the shelters on Cape Ann after I see how it works. Not to sound like an old lady," she said, stifling a yawn, "but I think I'm ready for some shut eye."

The others agreed, and after saying goodnight to Sharon, they ambled off through the park back to the Bed & Breakfast. Sharon listened to the giggles as she gathered the empty wine glasses. *I wish they could all meet Tim and Maggie, but another time. I hope the two of them are having a quiet night in Gloucester. No word from Peg, so I'll take that as a good omen.*

* * *

Seated in a bright room at the Caldwell Community Center Saturday afternoon, the ladies were ready to start painting by the time they started their second glass of wine. They claimed one of three tables in a full class led by local resident Cassie Durand.

"Cassie's a friend of Maggie's," Sharon explained. "She works part time here teaching art classes, and part time creating amazing crafts at a local gift store in town. I'll take you there tomorrow before we leave."

Jean continued to admire Cassie's samples. "Her paintings are gorgeous; I might buy one to bring home."

"Jeez, don't you have enough in your own studio?" Kelly jested.

"I saw one with the gazebo in the park with the Bed & Breakfast behind it. Thought it might be a nice reminder of our girls' weekend."

Betty Sue swished some green on her canvas. "I'm glad she gave us the option not to include a dog or cat in the painting. I've never been one for having pets, but I love the idea of fall trees. If it looks okay, I might even be brave enough to hang it in my living room."

Kelly took a sip of wine and picked up her own brush. "Here goes nothing. If I screw up painting Chianti, I'll just paint over it with a bunch of orange and yellow and make a pile of leaves. Jean, you should definitely do these at home. I bet Arlene could hook you up with someone at the Elks to paint the ocean views."

"Not a bad idea. I'll have to talk to Cassie afterwards for advice."

The ladies chatted as images took shape on each canvas, and by the time they lined up for a class photo, all were hooked. As other attendees left with new masterpieces, Cassie welcomed their help in gathering brushes. "I'm glad you all had fun. I had another one in Danvers last night at the shelter where I adopted Bella." She gestured toward one of her sample paintings of a Labrador Retriever in a pink pastel tutu. "I'm a dancer, and she loves the tulle, for some reason."

"She's beautiful." Jean admired her work up close. "Our friend Terri has two labs; she'd love this. I'm a retired art teacher, by the way, and I really appreciate your talent."

"Jean's thinking of running a few of these events herself – up on Cape Ann," Sharon said. "Maybe she can call you to pick your brain."

Cassie's eyes brightened. "Any time! If you were a teacher, you'll have no trouble filling the seats. I'm an Art Education major in school; might take forever with only one or two classes at a time."

"Because her two jobs keep her so busy." Sharon placed the last empty wine glass on a tray and picked it up. "I'll bring these into the kitchen and wash them for you. Will you be at Brooke's tomorrow? Have to bring the ladies in before they head home."

"You'll all *love* Brooke's shop. Something for everyone." Cassie grinned as she washed down the first table. "Don't spend all your money tonight."

Sharon laughed as she headed out the door. "Tonight, we feast. Can't invite the girls to town without a dinner at Gino's."

Cassie smiled. "You ladies are in for a treat – and probably lots more wine, too."

CHAPTER TWENTY-SIX

The next morning, Sharon made Carl breakfast before leaving. He sat at the kitchen table sulking with his crossword puzzle book. "Don't know why you're bothering with eggs; probably a peace offering so you don't feel guilty for abandoning me the whole weekend."

Sharon kissed his head as she placed the meal before him. "It was only yesterday, Dad." Sitting down next to him with coffee, she added, "They leave in a couple of hours, and then you're stuck with me for the rest of the day, so you better have something in mind for us to do."

Carl responded with a shrug of his shoulders, ignoring her as he ate. *You old curmudgeon; you're so damn possessive of your family. And I wouldn't have it any other way.* "It will be sunny and warm this afternoon. We could walk up the street to visit with Ida for a bit."

He remained silent, but she saw the smile creep onto his face. *You and Ida got to be such close friends while you were at the Manor for rehab; I'm glad you still spend time together.* She sipped her coffee, sure that Tim and Maggie were enjoying their weekend. Peg had texted the night before affirming Sean was with Tiffany the entire weekend. *No big surprise there. Enjoy your freedom, you two-timing skunk. Hopefully soon you'll be sitting alone in a jail cell.*

"What's that smile for?" Carl broke the silence at last.

"I was thinking about Tim and Maggie, and what a lovely weekend they've had."

"Why, 'cause they got away from me?"

Sharon laughed. "Hardly. But it's nice when married couples have some alone time, don't ya think? I bet you and Mom used to enjoy a little time away, didn't you?"

Carl sat back and sighed. "There's a place with rental cabins up on Lake Winnipesaukee we used to visit early in the season, before it got too crowded. Little spot right on the lake. Forgotten about it till now. Your mother was convinced you were conceived there, I might add."

"Now I'm intrigued – might have to find out if it's still around." She took Carl's empty plate as she stood. "Who knows? Maybe a great-grandchild will come along in the same manner."

"A baby? In this house? Oh, Lord, help me…" Carl turned back to his crossword puzzle shaking his head, but Sharon hoped he would live long enough to welcome another generation to Caldwell. *Let's not get ahead of ourselves. They've only been married a year, after all.* After washing the dishes, she assured Carl she'd be home to make him lunch and kissed him goodbye.

She spotted her friends packing the car in the distance, and quickened her stride toward the center of town. The ladies had agreed to meet her there, anxious to visit *Brooke's Treasures* before leaving for Gloucester.

"Oh, my Lord, this place smells like heaven," Betty Sue declared upon entering. "Is that Banana Bread?"

"One of the signature candle scents – all homemade. Speak of the devil," she added as the owner came down to join them, "Ladies, this is my friend Brooke Martin, who also helped Barb start the community garden I showed you yesterday. Brooke, this is Jean, Betty Sue, and Kelly."

"So nice to meet all of you; Sharon's told me all about her Gloucester visits. I hope you had fun in Caldwell."

"The best," Kelly replied. "Nothing like girls' weekends! And looking around, I suspect we might be here awhile. Your shop is gorgeous."

Brooke smiled. "Thanks; welcome to my home away from home. Take your time and browse away; there's something for everyone. Quite a few items were made by Cassie, and I heard you all spent time with her yesterday."

"We did," Jean said. "She's quite the talented artist."

Brooke agreed. "She's in the back if you want to say goodbye before you leave. Her pet themed gifts are selling like crazy, and we're able to help a few animals in the process."

"Well, don't you worry your pretty little head about that," Betty Sue chimed in. "Once Kelly finds that display, she'll be spending all her money. Surprised she didn't bring her little pooch along for the weekend."

"Next time," Kelly grinned. "But first I want to check out these candles that smell good enough to eat."

They took their time perusing all the items in the shop, and each of them had several items to purchase by the time they finished. "I knew you'd all love it here," Sharon teased. "Why don't we go in and say hello to Cassie before you ladies take off?"

Cassie wasn't alone in the back room, as Bella jumped up from her blanket in the corner to welcome them with a thumping tail. "She doesn't usually get visitors back here, aside from Brooke and a couple of friends. Settle down, girl. They're good people."

Kelly got down on her knees to welcome Bella's kisses, scratching behind her ears and above her tail. "What a sweet girl you are," she cooed.

Cassie laughed. "You've got a friend for life, now. I guess you ladies are heading home soon, huh?"

"Car's packed and waiting outside," Jean said. "But I'm glad we stopped in here – and did you paint all these yourself?" She picked up a wooden keychain with a terrier and "I love my dog" painted on it, and delicate paw prints as the border. Each one had a different dog or cat painted on them.

Cassie nodded. "I started them all last week; today I'm finishing with the paw borders. We sell a ton of these, and I'd taken a bunch to the shelter on Friday, so wanted to restock here. I'll be starting a whole set with black cats and pumpkins for our Halloween display later on."

"These are simply darling," Betty Sue said. "We'll have to ask Sharon to bring one of those up for Peg – doesn't she have a ton of black cats?"

"Five," Jean answered. "Plus, four orange tabbies – she'd go nuts with your pet display out here."

"Sounds like my kind of lady." Cassie was interrupted by her phone ringing. "Sorry, I need to take this– my friend Teagan only calls me at work with important stuff."

As she listened to her friend, she grabbed her computer and opened it. "Are you *kidding?* Okay, call you later!" She hung up quickly, super excited as she typed. "Sorry, ladies, but the Friday fundraiser is on one of my favorite blogger's channels. I can't believe it!"

As the ladies all crowded around behind Cassie, all but Betty Sue glanced at one another as they recognized Tiffany Henderson. She stood with a painting she'd completed with Cassie and various dogs in the background. "Can you believe I did this myself? Our *Paint for Paws* event was a huge success, and I have to *rave* about the talented artist who made it happen. Even though the party's over, we'll have a huge selection of artwork – painted by the talented Cassie Durand – available to buy all weekend, and every purchase helps another dog find its *fur-ever* home. Cassie and I both adopted our labs from here, and I hope you'll come to visit North Shore Lab Rescue this weekend!"

"I can't believe I made her channel!" Cassie sat transfixed.

"You better keep painting," Jean said. "She's got tons of followers."

The camera panned out to show a table displayed with Cassie's work, finally coming back to the blonde at the end. "I'm Tiffany Henderson, and that's my *rave* for the week!"

Cassie was about ready to close her computer when Betty Sue grabbed her arm. "Wait! Go back a second! Right after she finished!" Cassie, still shaking from excitement, fumbled with her mouse as Betty Sue leaned in. "It can't be!" she groaned. "But I swear it's Sean!"

"*Your* Sean?" Kelly asked.

Betty Sue pointed to the screen as Tiffany finished her rave and stepped into the arms of Sean McClean, who planted a huge kiss on camera while his hand reached around to pull her butt in closer. "Right there! But why is she kissing him like that?! He's *my* sugar bear!"

The excitement of Tiffany's rave came crashing down as all eyes stared at the unmistakable image of Sean and Tiffany frozen on screen. Cassie, sensing the situation, slipped to the side and excused herself. "I gotta go tell Brooke; I'll leave you guys alone."

Sharon almost followed her to apologize for ruining her moment, but decided to wait until they others had left. Betty Sue needed her more. Kelly had already wrapped an arm around Betty Sue's shoulders as Betty slumped onto a stool next to the table. "Honey, I hate to say it, but it's pretty obvious that Sean is cheating on you..."

"But she's younger...and *skinny!* How could he do that to me?" Tears spilled from her eyes, which remained on the couple before her. "I won't believe it – Sean loves me, I'm sure of it! He wants to buy a house, remember?"

Jean approached from the other side and rubbed her back. "Betty, I know you love him, but *look* at him – men don't go around groping another woman's ass unless they're getting a piece of it. Trust me, I speak from experience."

Betty wailed. "But Sean's different – he wouldn't do that to me!" Kelly and Jean let her cry, both remembering how disbelief collided with love and hurt when infidelity was confirmed. Sharon looked on, her own stomach churning. *Just another life you've destroyed, you asshole. Not to mention a perfect weekend. I can't imagine what their trip home will be like now. I only know I'm glad I won't be along for the ride.*

CHAPTER TWENTY-SEVEN

Jean spent the ride back to Gloucester in the back seat with Betty Sue crying on her shoulder most of the way. Once back to Kelly's, they changed cars and Jean drove her home, driving with one hand as Betty Sue clung to the other. "I was wrong! It wasn't him!" Betty Sue wailed. "He wouldn't *do* that to me!"

And here we go again. Round fifty-nine. Jean squeezed her friend's hand as they made their way down Stacey Boulevard. "Honey, we all saw him. I know it hurts like hell, but you'll get through it, I promise. We're all here for you." *We owe Tiffany a big thank you. You might never have to find out what we've all been up to.*

Wads of used tissues lined the floor as the sniveling continued. "But he *loves* me! He was gonna *propose* soon!"

Trying to maintain a sympathetic response was no easy task. "He only talked about living together," Jean pointed out, "And who knows if he was serious about that?"

Betty Sue pushed Jean's hand away. "Of *course,* he was serious! Are you implying that he was faking the whole time? Because I won't believe that!"

And now the denial and anger sets in. Believe me, honey, I understand. Jesus, Adam took off with my sister when the girls were so young, but those feel-

ings are never forgotten. I really wanted to kill him – both of them. She decided silence was a welcome option for the short ride remaining.

Once back at the townhouse, her sympathy returned. "I know you refused to stay with Kelly, but let me come in with you for a while," she offered. "We don't want you to be alone right now." Betty Sue objected at first, but changed her mind after retrieving her bag from the back seat. Jean helped her inside and poured a glass of wine for both of them, joining her friend who had curled up on the couch. "Drink this – it'll help."

Betty Sue nodded, taking a long sip before noticing the blinking light on her answering machine. "I bet he's called!" she blurted out, setting the wine down beside her as she hit the button.

"Hey, sugar, I'm missing those curves like crazy," Sean's voice dripped like sticky syrup, "But you picked a good weekend to spend with the ladies as I've been tied up in meetings all weekend. I'll call you later this week – by then I might have a *house* to show you, sugar."

"See?" Betty Sue was defiant. "It couldn't have been him! He's buying us a—"

Jean held up her hand to silence her as a second message had begun. "...manager from Keystone Bank. I'm calling to discuss some irregular activity in your account that caught my attention. Please call me at your earliest convenience. Thank you." Alarms went off in Jean's head as Betty Sue grabbed her cell phone. *Please tell me you didn't give that scoundrel any personal information. My God, this could be bad!*

"Probably some stupid scam," her friend assured. "Sean's always warning me about people trying to take my money....hmmm, that's odd...that *is* the right number for the bank...and it did sound like Dennis."

"You better call him," Jean instructed. "He'll at least call you first thing in the morning."

"I can't imagine what he'd want..." Betty Sue grabbed a sip of wine before dialing. "Dennis? This is Betty Sue Marino, returning your call. I'll be home all day Monday if you'd like to call, or I can stop in at the bank if you'd prefer." Ending the call, her hands fumbled a bit as she deliberated.

"Honey, don't call Sean back – not until you know for sure. If that *was* him in the video—"

"Well, then, he wouldn't have called me, now, would he?"

Jean sat down next to her and covered her friend's hands before she could dial. "But what if you're wrong? What if it *was* him, and he's been lying to you the whole time?"

"Why do you keep insisting that he's cheating on me?" Betty Sue demanded. "It was only a second or two on video, and there's no proof—"

"It was *him,* damn it!" *Shit. I didn't want you to find out this way. But I can't continue our little charade if you're thinking of ignoring this.* "Honey, Sean's not the dream man you think he is. We didn't want to tell you until we heard back from the police, but—"

"The *police!*" Betty squealed. "What do the *police* have to do with any of this? And who's *we?*"

Jean handed Betty Sue her own glass of wine. "You better drink more of this. I have a lot to tell you..."

* * *

Several hours passed, and Jean's calm and gentle manner helped to lessen the blow as she explained the timeline of what had become "Operation Sean Be Gone" to her friend. She patiently diffused the anger and disbelief first directed at her and the brunch club, and eventually led Betty Sue's emotions to the correct source. "Sweetie, none of us wanted you to be hurt like this. And we all promised each other to do whatever we had to do to protect you." Jean sighed. "I only hope we're not too late."

Betty Sue leaned back, exhausted from the roller coaster of emotions. "If I find out Sharon was wrong about any of this, I swear I'll never speak to any of you again. But, if she's right...my God, what if Dennis is calling to tell me..." She couldn't croak out the rest.

"We'll figure it out. All of us – we have your back."

"I'm just so tired. I feel so empty inside right now."

Jean patted her hand. "You need some sleep – if you think your brain could shut down."

"I think it already has." Betty Sue reached for the quilt on the back of the couch. "I'm gonna curl up right here – I don't think I can face the bedroom right now."

Jean tucked her in and took her phone. "I'm turning this off – as well as your landline." She gently kissed Betty Sue's forehead and stroked her curls. "Promise to call me first when you wake up, okay? Tomorrow I'll come back with whoever's free—so don't call Dennis until we arrive. We'll bring brunch, okay?"

"Don't forget the bloody mary," came the reply from inside the quilted cocoon.

Trust me, honey. That's the first thing I'll pack, and I'll make sure there enough for all of us, believe me. Let's hope Operation Sean Be Gone is entering its final phase.

CHAPTER TWENTY-EIGHT

The whole gang cleared their schedules when Jean started making phone calls, and even Sharon took the day off to drive up to Gloucester. She was the last to arrive, and when Kelly let her in, she could hear Betty Sue's sobbing. "Is it safe for me to come in? I don't want to make things worse by—"

"Is that Sharon?"

The sobbing had stopped, and Sharon slipped in. Betty Sue, with a slightly swollen face and smudged mascara, patted the seat next to her on the couch. Not sure what was about to happen, Sharon sat with distance between them and met her friend's gaze. "Please say you don't hate me."

Expecting another round of sobs, she was surprised when Betty Sue scooted closer and grabbed on to both of her hands. "Don't you worry your pretty little head about that," she sniffled. "If it weren't for you, he might have taken *all* my money."

Sharon hugged her friend as the tension between them dissipated. "I'm so angry he's destroyed another life...and so sorry you got hurt."

Kelly perched on the arm of the couch on Betty Sue's other side. "She's stronger than she thinks...and she's got all of us to help her through the tough times."

"I'm almost afraid to ask--any update from the bank?"

"That *skunk*!" Betty Sue spat out. "He managed to steal over a hundred grand from my accounts – thank God Dennis checks on them for me or I might have been screwed!" She reached for the tissue box on the table to find only one remaining tissue left. "I've gone through a whole friggin' box since last night!"

Jean got up from her seat in the corner. "There are several boxes still in your linen closet. Be right back. Sharon, can I bring you a glass of wine? We all started early."

"A small glass. Thanks." Still holding Betty Sue's hand, she settled back on the couch and scanned the room. "So, what's the status at this point?"

Even Arlene had a wine glass in her hands, and she nervously ran her finger around the rim as she spoke. "I think Mr. McClean is going to need a good lawyer – and it won't be my James, thank God. He doesn't do criminal cases."

Terri grinned. "Criminal. I like the sound of that. Peg, why don't you fill Sharon in."

"My pleasure," Peg replied, pausing to address Betty Sue. "Would it be easier if we went outside? I don't wanna put you through it all over again."

Although tears filled her eyes, Betty Sue nodded. "Go on. I'll be damned if he thinks he can keep hurting me..." Her words ceased as more sobs came, but she nodded toward Peg as she buried her face in her last couple of tissues.

Peg passed Sharon a manilla folder. "We had them on the table earlier, but she doesn't need them in her face—even if he did prove himself to be the ass we suspected."

Sharon opened the envelope and glanced through numerous shots of Sean with Tiffany throughout the weekend, including a few displaying lewd behaviors in public settings. "Not exactly discreet, is he?" Glancing toward her friend beside her, she added, "I'm so sorry you found out this way."

Jean returned with a new box of tissues and wine for Sharon. "Sean might have done us all a favor. I'm not sure our Southern Belle here would have accepted the rest of the story right away. Nothing beats stronger than a scorned heart."

"You'd certainly be one to know," Peg replied. "Someday, Sharon, we'll tell you the saga of Jean's deceased husband."

"My goodness, you make it sound like she did him in," Arlene chided. "He didn't die until years later."

Kelly opened the new box of tissues and handed Betty Sue more as the used wads accumulated on the rug. "Yeah, but several of us have lived through what Betty Sue's feeling right now. And we'll give her the same help we received."

"Not to change the subject," Sharon said closing the folder, "But where do we go from here?"

Peg reached over the table to take it. "I stopped by and met with the detective first thing this morning; I wanted to tell him about Tiffany in case Sean was stealing from her as well, and after going through all the files we handed him last week, his boss agreed there's enough probable cause for a warrant. They were contacting the Clerk of the Courts today, and a warrant may be out before the end of the day."

"Good!" Betty Sue hissed. "The bastard belongs in jail for what he's done!"

"Damn right," Kelly agreed, patting her back. "And I'm gonna have the pleasure of seeing his face when he's arrested. I called and told them I'll be showing him a house tomorrow morning, and they plan to be waiting outside when we're finished. I've never been so happy to lose a commission."

Another round of wailing began. "He told me it was gonna be *our* house..."

"You cry as much as you need to," Sharon whispered. "And think about how his new house will have bars instead of windows. I can't believe he's finally gonna get what's coming to him. I think we should *all* go tomorrow. Hell, I'll stay over so the whole brunch club can be there to support Betty Sue."

Jean lifted her glass. "Damn, that's a good idea. To Operation Sean

Be Gone...and to the friendships here that will last long after he's in jail."

Not even tears kept Betty Sue for joining in the toast. "Damn right. And I hope he rots there."

Peg snickered. "He's gonna look God-awful wearing orange. I hope we can manage a photo."

CHAPTER TWENTY-NINE

The following morning Kelly met Sean at a gorgeous ocean-front home on Eastern Point Blvd with meticulous lawns sprawling down to a private deep-water dock with a panoramic view of Gloucester Harbor.

Sean slammed the door of his Ford Fusion and grinned at the view. "Now this is what I'm talking about. Even better than the pics online."

Much as I'd like to push you off that dock, I'll behave for the next half hour. It'll be so worth the wait.

"Thanks for being right on time; I have an important meeting later and can only give thirty minutes for a quick tour. Hope that works for you."

Sean ran his hand along the masonry as Kelly unlocked the door. "Hell, I have a $200,000 check with me to hold this baby."

How much friggin' money did you steal from my friend? Or maybe you've been stealing from Tiffany as well, you bastard. "Why don't you go inside first, and afterwards we can discuss options." She swung the door open to allow him to enter, but instead Sean stepped in close and put his hand on her back.

"Ladies, first – always." Sharon almost gasped as Sean's hand moved lower while she entered. *Trying to touch my butt, now? Oh, you're such a piece of crap!* Resisting the urge to turn around and smack him, Kelly led him through the house, making sure to keep lots of distance between them.

Sean whistled when she led him into the master bedroom, complete with a deck overlooking the harbor. "Now that's a view I could get used to. Hell, it's even better with you standing right there—you are one mighty fine-looking woman, I must say."

Kelly's hair stood on end as Sean's gaze ran down her body. His voice lowered as he stepped toward her. "You must get lonely some nights living all by yourself. Your husband was stupid to leave a smokin' hot body like yours."

Kelly stepped back, making sure she was closer to the door than he was. *Police should be out there waiting at this point, so stay calm. He can't hurt you.* "Actually, I left *him*," she replied, trying to keep her voice steady despite the fear within. "He cheated on me – with one of my best friends."

Her words had the effect she'd hoped for, as Sean flinched before turning his attention to the view outside. "So...uh...how deep is the water by the dock?"

Yup, I hit a nerve, you scumbag. Her phone vibrated and she grinned inside as she scanned the text message: *All set outside.* "Will manage up to a forty-foot boat – after that it would be wiser to use one of the moorings or a local marina. Betty Sue never mentioned you owning a boat, Sean – what size is it?"

His lack of knowledge about technical aspects of sailboats was obvious as he stumbled over words. "Oh, I've been looking at a couple – different sizes -- and I think that dock would work fine."

Knowing the police had arrived renewed Kelly's confidence. "If you have any questions, I can help. My husband and I owned a boat—had a slip at the Harbor Side Yacht Club down in Salem. Nice little marina if you end up buying a place without a dock."

Another zinger. "I'll...file that away," Sean blurted out. "I think I've seen everything I need to. Exactly what I want."

Kelly stifled a chuckle. "I guess the only question left is whether you'd prefer bringing Betty Sue back to see it?"

Sean followed her down the curved staircase. "That would spoil the surprise, now, wouldn't it?"

Stopping in the foyer, Sean took one last look around as Kelly's anticipation grew. "The layout really is perfect for the four of you."

"Huh?"

"Well, the two bedrooms on this level would be great for Elena and Carla, giving you and Betty Sue some privacy upstairs."

"Right − of course!" Sean recovered in an instant, reaching into a pocket and pulling out a checkbook. "I absolutely want it! I have a check all written out for a deposit − all I need is a name."

Bingo! The account was for North Shore Handyman − and Kelly was certain he was paying with her good friend's stolen money. "Normally, I'd have you wait until the offer is in writing, but I spoke with the owner this morning and he said he turned down a lower offer last night, but would definitely accept the first one for full asking price. Why don't you make it out to Sea View Realty, and our attorney can hold it in escrow while I draw up the paperwork today. I'll call him from the car, and you should have yourself a house." She opened the door as Sean handed her the check, and led the way outside. "I'm sure Betty Sue will love the place."

Before Sean replied, two officers approached from around the corner of the house. "Good morning. Sean McClean?"

"Yeah, what can I do for you, officers?"

"We're placing you under arrest," the officer said, pulling out a pair of handcuffs. "Could you turn around please?"

Sean stepped back, as if his palms would keep the law at bay. "There must be some mistake—"

"Sir, we have a warrant for your arrest. Please turn around and put your hands behind your back."

Sean tried desperately to mask his fear. "Kelly, I don't have any idea what this is all about. Honestly."

As the handcuffs locked into place, she flashed a saccharine smile. "I don't know, Sean....did you do anything..." She held up the check he'd given to her. "...illegal?"

Her eyes met his, and she grinned. "He's all yours, officer."

"Wait? You're in on this?" Sean's temper flared as the officer turned him toward the street. "You bitch!" he hollered back over his shoulder. And then he saw them – the whole brunch club, surrounding a defiant Betty Sue, with Sharon by her side. Flustered, he stumbled for words. "Sugar...this...it's all a big *set up! Y*ou gotta believe me!"

Betty Sue approached with Sharon holding her arm for support. "Officer, may I please have a word with Sean before you take him away?" With their consent, she stood up straight and faced him defiantly. "Sugar, I will never believe another word that comes out of your mouth," she spat out. Stepping closer, she glared at her boyfriend. "I hope you rot in jail."

As her voice quivered, Sharon squeezed her shoulder, feeling free for the first time in years. "I'd say your past has come back to bite you, pal."

"You *bitch!*" Sean yelled. "You're behind all of this, aren't you?" As the officer opened the squad car, he continued his rant. "Soon as I'm out on bail, I'm driving to Caldwell to have a little talk with your *daddy!*"

Sharon couldn't stop smiling. "Yeah? Well, I'd advise you *not* to call Tiffany for bail money, as we had a lovely little visit with her this morning. Karma's a bitch, ain't it?"

Sean almost collapsed into the car, deflated by Sharon's revelation. "You'll be sorry! All of you!" The officer slammed the door shut with a little extra force. "I think he'll shut up pretty quick, ladies. They'll come by to pick up his vehicle. We'll take it from here."

Jean, Peg, Terri, Arlene, and Kelly joined the two of them as the squad car drove off. Betty Sue sobbed quietly while Sharon squeezed her arm. "You okay?" As Betty nodded and wiped her eyes, she added, "He can't hurt you anymore."

Kelly was the first to hug her. "And your money is safe, too, sweetie. I promise, you're gonna be okay."

Betty Sue turned to face the friends who had rescued her. Wiping her tear-stained face, she mustered a smile. "I don't know about you ladies, but I could use a drink. Anybody free for brunch?"

"If that's what you need, honey, then we're all here for you," Kelly promised. "Complete with a bloody mary for each hand. Let's head back to my place, shall we?"

CHAPTER THIRTY

Thirty minutes later, Kelly prepared a tray with croissants, fresh fruit, sliced tomatoes, lettuce, and seafood salad. Jean worked swiftly beside her mixing up the drinks. She opened the refrigerator in search of the final touch. "You have celery all sliced and ready to go? I'm impressed."

I *do* eat the stuff by itself," Kelly teased, "but I'm glad I got to the store and had all this here. Sounds like she's doing okay."

Up in the living room, Arlene and Sharon sat on the couch with Betty Sue between them, each giving comfort and back rubs when tears returned. Terri and Peg sat in wingback chairs, offering support from across the room. As the food trays arrived, even Arlene accepted a drink in support of her friend. "I believe God is okay with me having alcohol today. Betty, what should we drink to?"

With trembling lips, Betty held up her glass. "To friends – the only ones you can count on." She drank twice as much as all the others before the sobs returned. "It's true, you know. My boyfriend's going to jail, my mother's forgetting who I am, and my daughter hates me. You ladies are all I've got."

Sharon put down her drink and wrapped her arm around Betty Sue's shoulder. "And we'll all be here for you no matter what. But sweetie, I have to tell you, it's *never* too late to start over with your family. Believe me, I speak from experience."

"She's right," Arlene assured her from the other side. "I think you and Carla can still put the pieces back together again – even after all these years. I can't tell you how grateful I am to have JJ back."

Sharon continued on. "Two years ago, I was sure I'd be alone forever – but I took a chance, and have more than I could have imagined." Through tears, she added, "Maybe you can, too."

With assurances from all, Betty Sue sat in quiet reflection for a moment before sitting up straight. "You all know how much I hate being alone. I have no idea what I'm going to say, but I'm going to try reaching out to my daughter – and what's left of my mother."

Sharon raised her glass again. "I drink to Betty Sue reconciling with her family again. What do you say, ladies? What are you each drinking to?"

Arlene surprised everyone for speaking next. "For JJ to get his GED, and find a job he loves."

"I'll drink to finding respect at work," Peg offered. "And if my boss won't give it to me, I'm gonna quit and explore other options."

"You go, girl," Kelly said. "As for me, I'll drink to my marriage...and being brave enough to try again with Travis."

Terri was next in the circle, and she gazed at the floor as she spoke with hesitation. "To Vinny. And not losing him, too."

Jean patted her shoulder. "Don't worry. He'll come home."

"What about you?" Terri asked gruffly. "Your sister coming home?"

Jean stiffened as she leaned back in her chair. "Sorry, ladies, but no family reconciliation at this end." Looking back toward Terri, she raised her glass. "But I'll drink to Kim. That she might find love again."

Sharon, her heart full of love for these new friends in her life, turned to Betty Sue. "I guess that leaves only you, my dear. What are you drinking to?"

Betty Sue didn't hesitate. "To friends – you've been here for me my whole life, even when I deserted you and moved to Tennessee. You're the best people around, and you bring out the best in me while ignoring what a self-centered brat I am most of the time. And Sharon,

I might curse you out during the lonely nights ahead, but I'll also be forever in your debt for saving me from that bastard."

Kelly agreed. "You may live down in Caldwell, but I'm officially inducting you into the brunch club from here on. I'm sure everyone approves."

The clinking of glasses signaled confirmation, along with a cheer that lived within each of them – learned long ago as childhood friends who gathered on the beach and became family. Only one word was needed as they raised their glasses.

"Viva!"

Betty Sue Marino – She grew up in the same neighborhood as Terri Rossi and Jean McBride, and worked in the fish factory until she graduated from high school. She married young, becoming a mother at age 20, and after her husband split, she and Carla returned home to live with her mother Elena. Betty Sue married her new boss and left her daughter to travel the world with her new husband, who didn't want kids. After living many years in Tennessee, she returned home after Elena's dementia diagnosis.

Now a rich widow at age 51, she lives in a townhouse on the other side of the harbor from her mom and Carla. Her friends still call her out for her self-centered and impulsive choices, but love her regardless. She's a social butterfly who hates being alone, and book one is all about her latest boyfriend and her inability to reconnect with her mom and daughter. She may not be your favorite character in this book, but I promise she'll do a lot of growing in the future!

Her mom is Elena DiNardo (78), who suffers from dementia, and her daughter is Carla Douglas (28), who has lived with and cared for her "Nonna" since her mom left her behind.

As for Betty Sue's new boyfriend? Let's just say she doesn't have a great track record for choosing the right men. ☺

. . .

Jean McBride – Jean graduated from Gloucester High School with Terri. After getting married, she lived on the other side of town, but when her sister ran off with her husband, she moved back to her childhood home with her two daughters, Kim and Hannah, eventually inheriting the house. The girls are now both in their twenties, but live at home, and Jean is now retired after a career teaching art at the high school she attended.

She's down to earth, sarcastic, and independent. After some heartbreak in the early years, she's found her "family" in her friends and neighbors, and is still revered as a favorite teacher from past alumni. She loves to paint, cook, read, and spend time with her friends.

Her daughter Kim works as a music teacher, as well as an educator and event coordinator at nearby Hammond Castle. She lost her fiancé several years back, only two months before her wedding. She is just now beginning to wonder about dating again.

Jean's other daughter Hannah is a personal care assistant for Elena (Betty Sue's mother) during the day, but would love to someday run her own online business doing Tarot readings. She's a vegan, and dreams about someday living in her own tiny house.

Kelly Fitzgerald-Doyle (52) – She went to school to with Betty Sue, and spent lots of time down in her neighborhood where everyone felt like "family." After graduating from high school together, Kelly traveled to Boston for college, where she met her husband Travis. After 28 years of marriage, she discovered that her husband had been unfaithful to her, sleeping with her old college roommate while on a business trip. They've been separated ever since, and even though Travis is longing for a second chance, Kelly is afraid to trust him again. She works as a successful realtor in Gloucester, and in her spare time she enjoys jogging, knitting, reading, dancing, and sailing. She lives in a condo out by Bass Rocks with her dog Chianti.

. . .

Arlene Winston – At age 59, she's the quiet one of the group, and didn't become a real member of the brunch club until later in life. She's a submissive stay at home wife of James Winston, prominent lawyer, and she feels lonely in her marriage. Her hobbies give her peace at home, where she loves to knit, crochet, quilt, and read. Aside from activities at church and the Elks lodge, her only real social life is time spent with Kelly and the other brunch club ladies.

Her husband James is a misogynistic lawyer who expects his wife to be home to cook and clean. He pulled strings to keep his son out of jail on a drug arrest – mostly for his own image. I don't think he'll be anyone's favorite character. 😊

Her son JJ (James, Jr.) dropped out of high school and left town, only to return in the past couple of years with a drug problem. After being arrested, his father managed to keep him out of jail, and he now has a strict curfew at home as he completes his community service. He's 33 years old, committed to his recovery, and loves working with his hands, building and fixing things. His relationship with his mom is strained, as emotions aren't shared openly at home, but it's clear that they love each other.

Peg Fernandez – She graduated high school with Terri's husband Nate, and after secretarial school, she landed a job at the local newspaper, slowly working her way up to one of the top journalists on staff. Now at age 62, she frustrated as hell with a new boss who demoted her to cover community and social events. She owns nine cats, and loves news, police scanners, history, biographies, and Gloria Steinem.

She lives in her parents' old house over by Hammond Castle, and she has three young adults living with her to help make ends meet; one of them is JJ Winston, Arlene's son.

Terri Rossi – She grew up in the neighborhood with Jean and Betty Sue, and after marrying Nate, she moved to his place over on E. Main Street by one of the other fishing piers. She helps her husband with his boat while on land, and processes fish in the factory part-time during the day. She'll also help out at St. Peter's Parish and the Elks lodge frequently. She lost her oldest son Anthony when his fishing boat got caught in a storm, but loves the lone survivor of the wreck, Bill Peterson, as one of her own. Her younger son Vinny came out as gay shortly before Anthony's death, and Terri continues to struggle with church teaching on homosexuality, her husband's inability to reconcile with his only living son, and her own longing to have Vinny back in her life. Terri swears like a sailor and has a dry, gruff sense of humor. In her free time, she loves the New England Patriots, sitting on the beach, and the brunch club.

LOOKING AHEAD...

Return to Gloucester for book two as the brunch club explores reconciliation.

Betty Sue and Carla meet to discuss needed arrangements for Elena. Will these two women be able to reconcile after so many years of heartbreak between them?

As Kelly reaches out to Travis, does their marriage survive, or do other forces work against their efforts?

Terri and Nate face the biggest challenge of their marriage; will it reunite their family, or tear it apart?

While the brunch club is busy supporting each other, the younger generation has issues of their own.

Hannah enjoys her budding romance with JJ, Vinny extends an invitation to Bill, and after a lot of reflection, Kim decides it's time to try dating again.

Coming some time in 2023!

Finally, if you enjoy this story, please consider leaving a quick review online. Thanks so much!

ACKNOWLEDGMENTS

To Noel Sellon, cover designer, who takes my jumbled ideas and images and creates magic every time!

To Kimberly Bouris, for the perfect cover photo of Pavilion Beach – I envy you for living in Gloucester!

To Joe Novella and the St. Peter's Fiesta committee, for allowing me to begin my novel with the Greasy Pole Contest and the fiesta – Viva!

To my great uncle, Roland Anderson, retired Deputy Chief of Police in Weston, MA, for sharing his expertise on police procedure.

To those who helped with beta reading and editing — especially Cheryl, my critique partners Michelle and Jo, and my fellow authors from the Writers' Cafe — your input and camaraderie push me to improve my craft.

To my own brunch club friends—I am blessed to know and love you all!

Finally, to Bob, Beth, and Rebecca, who continue to be my reason for living.

ABOUT THE AUTHOR

Laurel Wenson's love of small-town life serves as inspiration for her stories about love and friendship that span generations. *The Harbor Cove Brunch Club* is the first novel of her new series set in the fishing town of Gloucester, MA. Join six middle-aged women as they rely on each other throughout life's challenges.

Laurel lives in Bethlehem, PA, with her husband, two daughters, and a frisky feline. She is a member of the Greater Lehigh Valley Writers Group and an avid participant in National Novel Writing Month.

Follow her on social media or visit her website at: laurelwenson.com

ALSO BY LAUREL WENSON

The Caldwell Series:

A Promise to Keep

A Heart to Heal

A Family to Cherish

A Place to Belong

———

Sets on a Shoestring:

How to Build Set and Props on a Limited Budget